The Householder

Amitabha Bagchi

FOURTH ESTATE • *New Delhi*

First published in India in 2012 by Fourth Estate
An imprint of HarperCollins *Publishers*

HarperCollins Publishers India, Cyber City, Building 10-A, Gurugram,
Haryana-122002, India
www.harpercollins.co.in

2 4 6 8 10 9 7 5 3

First published in paperback in 2013

ISBN: 978-93-5116-047-2

Typeset in 11/15 Galliard BT at
SURYA

Printed and bound at
MicroPrints India, New Delhi

MIX
Paper
FSC FSC® C218906

This product is made of FSC®-certified and other controlled material.

HarperCollins Publishers, Macken House, 39/40 Mayor Street
Upper, Dublin 1, D01 C9W8, Ireland

The Householder

Amitabha Bagchi is the author of *Above Average* (2007) and *The Householder* (2012), both of which were published to critical and popular acclaim. *This Place* (2013) is his third novel.

Praise for *The Householder*

'Amitabha Bagchi's second novel, *The Householder*, is a delight. And a welcome breath of fresh air in a literary atmosphere clouded with stylish feints and clogged with pretentious storytelling.'

– Arshia Sattar, *Open*

'Bagchi draws his characters with gentle compassionate strokes . . . *The Householder* makes old-fashioned demands of the reader: to get involved with the people, to will them on their way, to curse at the mistakes and smile at their achievements.'

– Arunava Sinha, *Mint*

'*The Householder* is a novel of brevity and force, one of the best this year.'

– Sunil Sethi, *Outlook*

For my father
Ajoy Bagchi
who was, among many other things,
a householder and an honest man

1

THE LATCH SCREECHED ON ITS SLOW WAY DOWN, THEN OPENED with a loud click. The door moved inwards, a dark slit appearing between its edge and the doorframe, but it did not open. Naresh Kumar fumed as he waited but the door stood in place, quivering, the hinges creaking with every microscopic motion.

'Open it,' Naresh called.

He needed to remind the CPWD maintenance office again to send someone to oil the hinges, he thought. When there is a nephew who needs a job, or a word to be put in for a promotion, they come running to me, but when there is work to be done in my house, there is always an excuse.

'What happened?' he asked, louder this time. 'Why aren't you opening the door?' He juggled his briefcase and the plastic bag overflowing with vegetables in a bid to get one hand free. Finally, he pushed against the door with his shoulder, a little harder than necessary, and it swung open.

'Just coming,' said Arti from the kitchen. 'My bhindi is burning.'

'Why did you lock the door?'

'Praveen has gone out somewhere,' came the voice from the kitchen. 'I'm alone in the house.'

Naresh walked to the dining table and dropped the plastic bag on it. The impact dislodged a lemon and three green chillies. The chillies lay where they fell, but the lemon rolled off the side of the table and down onto the floor, continuing on its merry way till it found a final resting place under the large fridge that stood just outside the kitchen. Naresh looked down, as if expecting the lemon to come rolling back out. Just one hour ago, he thought, he was in his chamber at the department, a place where people knew that he, Naresh Kumar, was the gatekeeper to Mr Asthana's office, an office where deals and contracts worth millions and billions of rupees were made and broken. And now here he was, having to go down on his knees and retrieve a lemon that had brazenly disregarded his status and decided to settle in an unreachable corner of the room. He took a deep breath – the air was redolent with slightly burnt okra – and turned and walked to the sofa.

'I need to talk to you about something,' said Arti, coming out of the kitchen. 'It's important.'

She was still attractive, Naresh thought, looking at the woman he had married more than twenty-five years ago. Layers of fat had appeared below her chin and on her midriff. Her arms jiggled as she walked. But the face that had fascinated him in those first few years was still there.

'Listen,' he said, collecting himself, 'I'm really fed up of carrying bags and bags of vegetables. We need a servant in the house, someone who can go to the market and get all this. We aren't that young any more.'

'You might be old,' she said, flopping down on the chair next to him, 'but I'm young enough not to want a boy loitering around the house all the time.'

'Uff,' said Naresh, shutting his eyes.

'And don't say we can get a girl, because we are not going to get a girl,' said Arti. 'Forget all that. I have something important to tell you.'

'What is it now?' asked Naresh, leaning back into the sofa. The exposed wooden frame hit his shoulder blade. Sitting back up, he glared at the sofa. With its richly polished wooden frame and tasteful paisley upholstery, this one large piece of furniture – bought after the only time Arti had been invited to Mr Asthana's expensively decorated home – dominated an otherwise quiet room's Formica-topped side table and government-issue wicker chairs. 'This sofa is worthless. Thirty thousand rupees and a tired man can't get any rest on it.'

'Leave the sofa alone,' said Arti. 'Everyone admires it. You should have seen Shanta's eyes widen when she saw it. Where did you get it? How much was it for? She kept running her hands over the wood.'

'What did you tell her?'

'What would I tell her?' said Arti. 'I said it was from a shop in Ghitorni. It cost thirty thousand rupees.'

'Your stupidity is going to destroy us one day,' said Naresh, in a tone more resigned than angry. 'Where does Shanta think we got the money for it? Here I am, still riding my old scooter all over the city when I could easily buy one of those big cars, just so the neighbours don't suspect anything, and you go around telling everyone that our sofa costs thirty thousand rupees. What next? Will you also tell them how many houses we own and how much land? How much jewellery you have in the locker and what it's worth? I haven't collected all this so that you can show off to your friends. It is there to secure our future, not to be put on display.'

'Okay, okay,' said Arti. 'There is no need for a long lecture. And let Shanta think what she wants. Her husband is not washed in milk either.'

'That's true,' said Naresh, smiling at the thought of Shanta's husband, or himself, bathing in milk. The impromptu inventory of the assets he had collected over the years had put him in a good mood.

'Listen,' she said, 'will you let me say what I wanted to say? There is something important.'

'More important than giving your tired husband his evening cup of tea?' asked Naresh. 'Or do you want me to make it myself? Maybe I can make you a cup too. One teaspoon sugar, or are you trying to lose weight again?'

'Sorry, sorry,' said Arti, getting up in a hurry. 'How stupid of me.'

'That's what I was also saying,' said Naresh. 'You are very stupid.'

Arti looked down at her husband. His trousers were fraying at the edges. This pair has to be discarded, she thought. When he slouched his stomach pushed his shirt upwards in an unseemly manner. She smiled. Then she leant forward, bringing her face close to his. 'If you talk too much nonsense,' she said, 'I'll put salt in your tea instead of sugar.'

'Go get my tea,' said Naresh imperiously. He was also smiling.

When Arti returned, two cups of tea in hand, her face was grave. 'Listen,' she said. 'It is a serious matter.'

'What is it?'

'Shanta came over this afternoon.'

'You already told me that,' said Naresh, taking a sip of his tea.

'She was saying that her brother, you know, that Anil who she had suggested should marry our Seema ...'

'Useless fellow. I wouldn't marry my worst enemy's daughter to him.'

'Anil saw Praveen,' said Arti, moving to the edge of the chair as she delivered this fact.

'Saw Praveen?' said Naresh. 'So what? I see Praveen everyday. I can go into his room right now and see him, snoring loudly as always.'

'I told you he has gone out. That's why I am telling you this now. Anil saw Praveen at the new mall in Saket. Shanta said that Anil was going to go and say hello to him when he saw that he was sitting there with some girl. A foreigner girl. Praveen was sitting in the mall with a foreigner girl.'

'So what?' said Naresh, exaggerating the irritation in his voice to hide his growing apprehension. 'In this call centre business all the clients are in foreign countries anyway.'

'The clients are in foreign countries,' said Arti. 'What are foreigners doing here?'

'Sometimes foreigners also come to India. Maybe she works in his company.'

'Listen to the whole thing first,' said Arti. 'Anil said that he was standing there trying to decide whether to say hello to Praveen or not. Just then a man came up to the table where Praveen was sitting. He sat down at the table and handed something over to Praveen. Praveen got up, leaving the girl and the man together, and walked away. He walked straight past Anil. He didn't even look at him.'

Naresh put his tea down. His right hand rose to his chin, fingers grazing over the light stubble that had emerged in the course of the day. 'So?'

'So? Just shut your eyes to the truth. Maybe it will become a lie.'

‘I am not the one who is trying to make the truth a lie,’ said Naresh, his voice rising. ‘It’s that Anil who is lying.’

‘Why would he lie?’

‘We rejected his proposal for our daughter, didn’t we?’

‘That was many years ago. He is happily married now.’

‘Hmph.’

‘In fact, he has one son already running around the house and another child on the way. Our daughter, on the other hand, can’t even …’

‘Can’t what?’ snapped Naresh, anger flooding his face. ‘She can. And she will. You may not think she will. But I know she will.’

‘You’re right,’ Arti said softly. ‘She will.’

The contrition in her voice, so rarely heard, drained the anger out of Naresh. He hesitated for a moment, then said, ‘What were you saying about Anil?’

‘No, I was just saying that Anil has no reason to lie about this.’ The diffidence in her voice was her way of thanking her husband for accepting her unsaid apology.

‘Does he even have a job that can pay for his family?’ asked Naresh, signalling a return to normalcy by deliberately speaking in the querulous voice used for everyday arguments.

‘Yes, he does,’ said Arti, gratitude replaced with combativeness as she settled back into the argument over Anil’s credibility. ‘In a big company. It’s a respectable job. Everyone has a respectable job except our son. Everyone goes to work at nine in the morning and leaves work at five-thirty, but our maharaja goes to work at ten at night and comes back at seven in the morning. God knows what he does all night, what kind of women he goes to the mall with and what else he does while we are sleeping.'

'You don't complain when he buys you gifts. He eats off my salary and buys his mother expensive earrings with his own.'

'The same raag again …' Arti said, her right hand rising involuntarily to her ear to touch the earring in question. 'Listen to what I am saying. Our son is getting involved in all kinds of things. If this continues, something bad will happen.'

'You should have thought about that when he was a child. Always spoiling him, buying him everything he asked for. I told you then that he will grow up not valuing anything. He will think that everything in life comes easily. I told you hundreds of times. But you didn't listen. My darling son! My only son! My beautiful son! Now you take care of your son.'

'And what have you been doing?' said Arti, the pitch of her voice rising further. 'I told you when he was finishing college, find him a proper job. Am I the only one who has to worry about him? What about your responsibility as his father? Have you forgotten your responsibility?'

Naresh put his cup down on the table. He stood up and walked to the fridge, opened it, looked inside, then slammed the door shut. Turning back, he said in a low quivering voice: 'I have not forgotten my responsibility. I have never forgotten my responsibility.'

Arti rose from the sofa and walked up to him. She put her hand on his shoulder. 'Don't get angry,' she said in a soothing voice. 'I didn't mean …'

Naresh brushed her hand off his shoulder. 'I know what you meant.'

Arti smiled and cupped his right cheek in her recently spurned hand. 'You have always provided for me. You have never forgotten your responsibility.'

'Hnnh!' But he didn't remove her hand.

'Will you do something about this?'

'I will. Let me see what I can do.'

'Sharmaji, namaste,' said Naresh Kumar, bending from the waist, his hands pressed together in front of him, as he went forward to greet his daughter's father-in-law. 'Congratulations!'

Sharmaji had a mobile phone pressed to his right ear. He brought his left hand up in half a greeting, then waved Naresh, Arti and Praveen on with that same hand. He nodded at them, but did not smile. 'Thank you ji,' he said, but from the upward tilt of his neck, it was clear that the person he was thanking was on the other end of the phone line.

When Naresh and his family walked through the saffron and yellow gateway, dodging hanging strings of marigold, they found the wedding enclosure buzzing with people: men in long embroidered kurtas or poorly fitting suits, destined to be worn only at such gatherings; women in synthetic saris with shiny sequinned patterns on them, selected after much discussion, not to be worn again when the same people were likely to attend.

The poorly maintained rectangular DDA park had been dressed up for the occasion. On one of its long sides were the chaat, golgappa, chilla, tikki and other fast food stalls whose function was primarily to keep people fed till the wedding procession arrived. Behind these, between the cloth walls and the white tent's roof, was a gap through which the housing colony that surrounded the park was visible in the last of the evening's light, its boxy stucco regularity punctuated by whimsical tiling or a coloured glass extension or by a clothesline whose washing was yet to be removed. The lights had not yet come on within these flats, nor would they till dinner had been served: Ashok's father, the host of his nephew's wedding, had invited each one of his neighbours. Nothing less was expected from the father of a sub-divisional magistrate. Across from the chaat counters, along the other long side of the park, were tables with large metal food warmers on them. Dinner would be served in these. Their paraffin heaters were ready but not lit; they would not be lit till the wedding procession arrived, a point of time in the indefinite future.

'Seema!' called Arti, hailing her daughter, who stood near a group of women but didn't seem to be talking to them. Seema turned to look. Her face brightened at the sight of her mother.

'This sari looks beautiful on you,' said Arti, hugging her daughter, then stepping back and looking her up and down. 'I told you it would look good. You have the complexion for it. And why aren't you wearing the diamond set I gave you? If you don't wear it at a wedding, and that too your own husband's cousin's wedding, then when will you wear it?'

'How are you, Mummy?' said Seema, smiling.

Seema touched Naresh's feet and tousled Praveen's hair. 'What is this sticky stuff you put in your hair, Bhaiyya?' she asked, wiping her hand on his tight jeans.

'Mummy,' said Praveen, 'she's ruining my jeans.'

'Uff,' said Arti. 'You are both grown up now. Still behaving like children.'

A corner of Naresh's mouth twitched upwards in amusement, but he brought it under control. 'I don't see our son-in-law.'

'He was just here,' said Seema unconvincingly, a shadow falling over her eyes.

'Did you get the report for the third round?' asked Arti.

'It came yesterday,' Seema replied, looking away from her mother.

'Why didn't you tell me?'

Naresh and Praveen waited, along with Arti, for the answer to this question, but Seema's head was turned. Her eyes appeared to be fixed on something in the distance.

Arti ran her hand over her daughter's head. 'Come,' she said. 'Let's eat some golgappas. It's been a long time.'

The two of them walked away, leaving Naresh and Praveen alone. A waiter passed by, carrying a tray of small glasses with variously coloured liquids in them. Praveen stopped him, choosing a cola drink. Then he turned and, seeing Naresh looking at him expectantly, turned again, tapped the now departing waiter on his shoulder and lightened his burden by one more glass.

'Praveen,' said Naresh, taking the glass from his son, 'your Mummy is a little worried about you.'

'That's not breaking news, Babuji,' said Praveen, sipping his cola while he sized up the women of various ages parading around the enclosure in their finest.

'No,' said Naresh. 'I'm serious. Someone told her they saw you in a mall with a foreigner girl.'

Praveen turned towards his father. 'Who told her that?'

'How does it matter who told her?' said Naresh. 'The question is: were you in a mall with a foreigner girl or not?'

'Tell Mummy not to listen to such nonsense,' said Praveen.

'Look, Praveen,' said Naresh, his voice hardening. 'I'm asking you a simple question. Were you in a mall with a foreigner girl or not?'

'Yes, I was,' said Praveen. 'Her name is Ella. She works at Infinix with me.'

'What does she do there?' asked Naresh.

'She is a voice trainer,' said Praveen. 'Our clients were complaining that their customers can't understand the accent, so they got an American girl for voice training.'

The idea that a call centre in Gurgaon could simply 'get' an American, and a woman at that, took Naresh outside the otherwise capacious realm of claims whose truth or falsehood he could readily verify.

'I think it's time you left this call centre job,' he said.

'And do what?' asked Praveen. 'Sit in an office for nine hours wearing out the nib of a pen?'

Praveen's cruel statement found its mark. Naresh, wilting within, looked at the boy's agitated face. Despite the spiked hair, tight jeans and insouciant slouch, there was still that face, that reminder of Naresh's own father whose nose was just like Praveen's – wide, pockmarked. And for a moment, it felt like his own father had delivered this crushing indictment of his life. What an incongruous idea, thought Naresh. It was, after all, his father who had informed him one day that this was what he was going to do for the rest of his life.

'Sorry, Babuji,' said Praveen, contrition in his eyes as they scanned his father's hurt expression. 'I didn't mean it like that.'

'If I find you something good, will you leave the call centre?' asked Naresh, collecting himself.

'Yes,' said Praveen, hanging his head, and Naresh knew that this acquiescence came only from the guilt the boy was feeling.

'Look,' said Naresh, 'I don't want to interfere in your life. As long as I'm there, I'll take care of you. After that, it is you and your destiny. But your mother thinks differently.'

'What are father and son whispering about?' asked Arti, as she approached them, two plates loaded with chaat in her hands. Seema came with her, smiling weakly. A small black shadow had formed at the corner of her right eye, but no one who was more than a foot away would have been able to tell that her eye liner had run and then been hastily dabbed with the end of a sari.

'I'll find your son-in-law,' Seema said, and walked away towards the gate, adjusting her sari's pallu on her head as she went.

Arti's eyes followed her daughter's retreating back. Naresh's eyes tried to read his wife's face. 'Is everything okay?' he asked finally.

'No, Nareshji,' Arti replied with a sigh, 'nothing is okay.'

Naresh started. Praveen too lifted his face from his plate of chaat. The two men stood there, waiting for Arti to say something that would justify the extreme step of addressing her husband by his name. But she said nothing, wordlessly digging into the mountain of chaat that sat on her plate.

'So what if the third round has failed,' said Naresh, his confident, tetchy tone concealing the anxiety that was beginning to spread within. 'We knew right in the beginning that this test-tube procedure has a low chance of success. We'll go to another hospital, a better one. I am not one to give up.'

'You may not be, but not everyone is like you.'

'What are you trying to say?'

'I had thought that maybe …' Arti turned to face the two of them. 'I had thought that I would tell her today to ask our son-in-law to find this boy a job. But I don't know if that is any use.'

'I don't need a job,' Praveen whined.

'Why don't you tell me clearly what has happened?' asked Naresh, ignoring Praveen.

'She doesn't say anything. On the phone she always sounds so happy. He brought me this today, he took me there today. My mother-in-law cooked this for me, my mother-in-law showed me that. But here, look at her, wandering around the pandal all alone.'

'And did you see how her father-in-law greeted us?' asked Praveen.

'He was talking on the phone,' said Naresh.

'Don't make excuses,' said Arti. 'There is something wrong.'

'I was just …'

'We were eating golgappas,' Arti interrupted him. 'I kept saying, don't worry, we will try again, we will go to a better hospital. And she said, I don't know, Mummy, I don't know how much more time I have left.'

'How much more time? She is only twenty-six.'

'I said the same thing. And she said, that's not the time I am talking about, and I saw that water was streaming out of her eyes. When I asked her why she was crying, she said she wasn't, she said some masala caught the back of her throat.'

'Maybe it did.'

'Hmph.'

Neither her husband nor her son responded. The chattering of the people who milled around heightened the silence that fell between the three of them as they stood looking in the direction that Seema had gone.

In the early eighties, Naresh's father had informed him that he had to study for the competitive exams to enter the government's clerical services. The Central Secretariat Stenographers' Service was the one he was particularly keen on. 'If you can't become an officer, the next best thing is to be an officer's doorkeeper,' he had said. 'If nothing else, you can make money by refusing to open the door.' But Naresh didn't study hard enough and could only make it to the clerical cadre of the Delhi government. The job was in Delhi, so he had to move away from home. This unexpected gift of personal freedom was not one he accepted gratefully. He found himself in Delhi, eating insipid vegetables he had to cook for himself in an old kadhai discarded by his mother and making fat undercooked rotis on a cracked tawa. A week into his new life, he wrote to his father saying he needed a wife.

A month later, his father sent him a thick envelope full of photographs. These were the girls whose horoscopes matched Naresh's and whose families' resources matched Naresh's father's expectations. It took Naresh five minutes to decide that Arti was the one he would marry; there was a little crook at the corner of her smiling mouth that beat out the other ten photographs and linked her destiny with Naresh's for the rest of their lives. Naresh wrote back to his father and received in reply, ten days later, a letter explaining that the dates and venues for the marriage ceremonies had been fixed. There was also a list of dowry items attached. The scooter and desert cooler at the top of the list – just below a plot of land that was going to be transferred to Arti – met with Naresh's approval, but the various items of domestic use that followed didn't mean much to him, so he skimmed over them, going straight to the bottom where a cash amount was mentioned.

The first thought that came into Naresh's head when he saw the number was that it was too small. He could have daughters too, he thought, their dowry would have to be arranged. He had a good job now and his salary was satisfactory, but what if something happened to him? What if he met with an accident, or fell ill and could not work? His irritation at the insubstantial figure grew into a full-fledged fear, a fear whose source he could possibly have traced to stories published in newspapers or disseminated through neighbourhood gossip. But a young man contemplating the dawning of adulthood is not as concerned with the provenance of his fears as he is with the means of assuaging them. So he wrote to his father saying that the money was not enough. A man must provide for his family, he said. The duty that comes before all duties is to strive for the happiness of his wife and his children. He didn't need cooking utensils, he had those already; he wanted more money so that his unborn children's future could be secured. Both his father and his father-in-law approved of the sentiment and, without consulting his mother or his mother-in-law, the list was revised. By the time Arti entered her new house, carrying just two brass platters and some silver drinking glasses, her heart sinking at the sight of the motley assemblage of worn second-hand pots and pans in the kitchen, the desert cooler had been installed, the new scooter had been registered in Naresh's name, and the money her father had given – more than double what he had initially offered – had been invested in government securities and fixed deposits.

One night, the third week in their new home, after he had praised her cooking, Arti showed Naresh the marks on her hands where the old kadhai had singed her and told him she needed a new one. They make them with wooden handles now, she had said. It makes life much easier.

On his way back from work the next day, Naresh stopped at Kotla market. They had kadhais with wooden handles, he was told, and they were priced from fifty-five rupees upwards. 'Best quality. Imported.' He went to four different shops, but there wasn't a single kadhai of a reasonable size below seventy rupees. The following weekend, he set off early and drove north to Sadar Bazaar. He spent an hour going from shop to shop, but not a single shop could show him a kadhai with wooden handles for less than sixty rupees. From there, he went to Chandni Chowk's Azad Market, where the price was not a rupee lower. It was almost lunchtime when a shopkeeper, perhaps taking pity on this harried customer, suggested that he could think of going to Wazirpur in West Delhi where the wholesalers and manufacturers were located. Another weekend, another long drive, another round of shops, and Naresh had run into a brick wall. The kadhais with wooden handles weren't made in Delhi – not enough demand; the ones in the shops were all imported. And each time he returned home and told Arti that he was not going to spend sixty rupees for a kadhai, she would make a face and fall silent. I'll find you a good kadhai at the right price, he would say, but she would not respond, and eventually he would change the topic.

It had been a month since his last foray into a utensil market when a woman came up to his table in the office. She was wearing an old and faded sari, its pallu drawn over her head. In the parting of her largely grey hair, there was an untidy sprinkling of sindoor. Shining out of her otherwise faded appearance, it looked like an afterthought. She was carrying some soiled papers in her hands – gnarled hands, their skin wrinkled and bunched up. Her husband had been a sweeper in the department. He had retired some years ago and was entitled to a pension. But he was ill and hadn't been able to appear in person to collect his pension, so it had not been paid for three months.

'A rule is a rule,' Naresh said. 'If he doesn't come, he cannot be paid. What can I do?'

'He is in bed,' the woman said, her face contorting, then righting itself as she spoke. 'The doctor doesn't know when he will get up.' She held out a scrap of paper with something scrawled in Urdu. There was no stamp, no letterhead.

'This won't do,' Naresh said.

'But this is what the doctor gave me.'

'I wasn't born yesterday,' Naresh said. 'There are a lot of people coming here, trying to get a dead man's pension.'

She flinched. 'Babuji,' she said. 'He is not dead. I have been coming here for six weeks. I scour dishes in three houses. If I miss one day, they cut my salary. The medicines are very expensive. I need the pension.'

Tears were welling up in her eyes. Naresh, new in government service and not yet hardened, told her to wait and took her papers to the section officer. He looked at the papers, particularly at the doctor's certificate. 'We can issue her voucher,' he said, 'but it's lunchtime now. And after lunch I need some tea.'

On the section officer's table sat a small glass half-full of tea. Naresh looked down at it, puzzled. He made as if to point to it, then decided not to. 'I'll tell her to come back at three,' he said.

The section officer looked up at him, amusement gleaming in his eyes. 'But I can't do her work till I have had my tea.'

Naresh looked again at the glass on the table, but it did not reveal the meaning of this cryptic pronouncement.

'Has she brought us something for tea?' the section officer asked finally, a broad smile on his face. That smile opened a lock in Naresh's mind.

'Yes,' he said, his hand reaching into his pocket. 'She has.'

The section officer took the banknotes that were handed to him. He didn't count them. 'Accept it pending confirmation, and forward it to me for approval,' he said. 'Don't take this medical certificate. Issue the voucher yourself.'

Naresh walked back slowly to his table, not sure what had just happened. He found the woman sitting on her haunches by his chair. He motioned to her to stand up. Throwing her papers down on his table, he loudly dragged his chair forward and sat down.

'You people don't know anything about rules and procedures,' he grumbled loudly, opening the pension register. 'Just come here with whatever useless documents and ask for pension. I also have to answer to someone, don't I?' He made an entry in the register, then pulled out the voucher pad from his drawer. Looking up, he saw an expectant look in her eyes. He put his pen down. 'What have you brought with you?'

'I gave you all the papers.'

'Have you brought anything apart from the papers?'

'What is there apart from the papers?' she asked, a hint of irritation in her voice.

'If you want to wait another six weeks for this money,' he said, giving her a contemptuous look, 'I can arrange that as well.'

She folded her hands in front of her chest. 'I didn't mean to offend you, Babuji. I really don't know what I should have brought apart from the papers.'

'Did your hair grow white from standing in the sun?'

She frowned, then her brow cleared and her eyes dropped. Her hand went to the corner of her pallu. She undid a fat knot at the end of it and brought out a tightly folded set of notes. She counted them slowly. Naresh counted along with her. She had some fifty rupees, mainly in one and two rupee notes, twenty more than he had given the section officer. When she was done counting, she held the money out. 'Leave it on the table,' Naresh said, picking the pen up and looking down at the voucher pad.

That evening, he stopped again at Kotla and bought for seventy rupees the kadhai with wooden handles that he could have bought for sixty in Sadar Bazaar. The next morning he pulled out his notes from the stenography classes he had taken in preparation for the exams. The following year, he resigned his job and entered the Central Secretariat Stenographers' Service.

Naresh looked up when he heard the door hinge creak. A square face poked into the room, the antechamber to Mr Asthana's office, where Shri Naresh Kumar – PA to Shri R.K. Asthana, Joint Director – and Shrimati Pinki Kaur, Stenographer, sat. It was a room with two doors of unequal importance. The less important door was the one that faced the gloomy corridors of the office building. This door was now opening to reveal the face of Mr Khanna, trusted sidekick to Mr Vinod Bhan, the chairman and managing director of several companies that were being referred to in the press over the last few years as the Bhan Group. The more important door – next to which Naresh's table was strategically located – was the one that led into Mr Asthana's office.

'You don't worry, please,' said Khanna into his phone, raising his free hand to Naresh. Under his right arm, he was carrying his usual leather pouch and an oblong object sheathed in a plastic bag emblazoned with Aggarwal Sweets' promise of eternal freshness and the name, phone number and address of their various locations. 'Yes, yes,' said Khanna. 'I have talked to Bhan Saheb. You don't worry. It will be done. Yes. Thank you ji. Thank you.'

Once the phone was safely tucked into the pocket of his grey safari suit, Khanna folded his hands. 'Namaste Nareshji,' he said. Pinki looked up from her magazine, but no greeting seemed to be coming her way.

'Mr Khanna,' said Naresh, pointing expansively to the chair across his table, 'come.'

'How are you, Nareshji?' asked Khanna, putting the Aggarwal Sweets packet on the desk.

'One second,' said Naresh, who had begun reading a document very carefully as soon as Khanna appeared. He wrote a few words on it, then ostentatiously opened a drawer and slipped the document in. With the air of a person who is satisfied with the task just completed, he looked up, brought his hands together and said, 'What can I do for you, Mr Khanna?'

'You shouldn't work so much, Nareshji,' said Khanna, slipping easily into his own role in this little charade. 'It's not good for the blood pressure.'

Naresh leant back in his chair and smiled, his mouth curling up at one end. 'If a working man won't work, then what will he do?'

'He will eat sweets,' said Khanna, taking a large rectangular box out of the plastic bag he was carrying. 'It was Mr Bhan's son's birthday on Sunday. He has sent this for you.'

Naresh took the box from him. From its heft he deduced that it could be either sweets or banknotes packed tightly. 'There was no need for this.'

'You and Mr Asthana are like family to Bhan Saheb,' said Khanna. 'Both of you have helped us so much.'

It was more than two years now since the government had decided, after careful political manoeuvring, that the nation's steel-producing capability needed to be augmented by opening three large scrap-processing plants. And that the privilege of building and operating these facilities would not be exclusively granted to public sector organizations. They would be operated by the player who made the best bid in an open process. This process was being conducted by the department Naresh was employed in. The officer handling the deal, reporting directly to the minister, was Mr Asthana. And one of the primary bidders for this deal was the Bhan group of companies.

'What have I done to help you?' said Naresh, putting the box of sweets down on one side of his desk. 'I have done nothing.'

'Nareshji, you are very modest,' said Khanna. 'After all, when the environmental sub-committee was formed …'

'Forget all that,' said Naresh, his eyes darting towards Pinki. Then, raising his finger silently towards Khanna as if to say 'one minute', he turned to her. 'Pinkiji,' he said, 'Personnel hasn't sent the file Mr Asthana had asked for. If we don't go and stand on their heads, they will not release it. And if I send Ram Prakash, they'll make some excuse and send him back.'

'I'll go, Nareshji,' said Pinki, folding her magazine shut.

'Don't accept any of their excuses,' Naresh said.

'I won't, Nareshji,' said Pinki, giving him a broad smile.

'Pinki is not one to be fooled easily,' said Naresh, addressing Khanna.

'Namaste, Pinkiji,' said Khanna, not embarrassed at delivering the greeting several minutes after it had fallen due.

Once Pinki had left the room, Khanna came to the point. 'Asthana Saheb has moved the note on dezincing to the minister.'

'I know,' said Naresh. 'I typed it myself.'

The problem was that one of the other bidders for this deal, the Vijay Group, had submitted a stronger bid, undercutting the Bhan Group's deal by almost six per cent. Such a large gap would ensure that the Vijay Group won out when the final scrutiny of bids took place. The only option was to have their bid disqualified. And Mr Bhan and Khanna had a plan in place for that disqualification.

The environmental sub-committee's report had been disregarded by the government, but it contained a minor and, from the Bhan Group's point of view, vital suggestion. The sub-committee had recommended that the process for scrap dezincing be compliant to the stringent European standard that had been recently announced. The Bhan Group, advised by Mr Asthana, had tailored its bid accordingly. The Vijay Group had disregarded this recommendation and come up with a proposal that complied with an American standard that was now fifteen years old. It was a calculated risk. The Vijay Group was hoping perhaps to argue that the new standard made the whole venture infeasible. To be on the safe side, their bid had included provisions for retrofitting the plants to meet the new standard once the technology became cheaper: a clearly hollow promise designed to express sincerity. With this in place, the Vijay Group was confident of winning the bid. But Mr Bhan was determined to stop them. The plan was that Asthana would reactivate the environmental sub-committee's report. The lacuna in the Vijay Group's proposal would be highlighted. The Vijay Group would be disqualified. There were three small-time bidders apart from the Bhan Group and the Vijay Group, so it would still appear like an open contest with multiple competitors. The Bhan Group would be awarded the contract.

'I have brought some papers for Mr Asthana,' said Khanna, unzipping his pouch. 'He said I should give them to you.'

Naresh took the papers he was proffered and looked through them. One set of documents was for a penthouse apartment in a luxury development that the Bhan Group was building in Gurgaon. These were made out in the name of Mr Asthana's son-in-law. The other set of papers confirmed Mrs Asthana's ownership of a plot of land in a newly designated township on the way to the airport in Bangalore. Satisfied that everything was in order, Naresh put the papers in a small safe he kept under his table. 'These are okay,' he said.

'Please give my regards to Asthana Saheb,' said Khanna, rising to his feet.

'Sit for a minute, Khanna Saheb,' said Naresh in a cajoling tone. 'Will you have some tea?'

'I just had some before I came,' said Khanna, sitting back down slowly.

'How is Bhan Saheb?' asked Naresh, an earnest expression on his face, his tone ingratiating.

'He is fine,' said Khanna, his brow furrowing as he tried to figure out why Naresh Kumar was extending this meeting.

'He is a great man. What an empire he has built! And that too single-handedly.'

'Single-handedly,' echoed Khanna. 'A big empire.'

'And do you know how he has done it?'

'How?' asked Khanna, taken by surprise at this sudden turn in the conversation that cast Naresh as the expert on all things Bhan and himself as the novice.

'By taking care of his people,' said Naresh, leaning forward and bringing his hand down on the table to drive home the point.

'Very true, Nareshji. Mr Bhan thinks of everybody. That's why, when he told me to deliver the papers to you, he said, also take some sweets for Naresh Kumarji.'

So there are banknotes in the box, thought Naresh. Just one box of cash. He wants to buy me cheaply. He picked it up now, Aggarwal Sweets plastic bag and all, and handed it across the table, back to Khanna. 'The doctor has told me not to eat sweets.'

'But Bhabhiji can eat sweets,' said Khanna, reluctantly taking the box.

'She doesn't like sweets. The only one who eats sweets in my house is my son. But that poor boy's stomach is always bad. All night he works in a call centre. Every night he is awake. How can the stomach take it?'

'It is difficult,' said Khanna absently, his mind ticking with the realization that he was in the middle of a negotiation.

'Now, if he had some job that he could do in the daytime, his health would return. After all, he is only a boy, just some twenty-two twenty-three.'

'Yes, yes,' said Khanna, relieved that the demand was so modest.

'Maybe if he had his own shop,' said Naresh, before Khanna could speak further. 'After all, this is the era of business. In these times, a person can only progress if he has a business.'

'You are right,' said Khanna, growing thoughtful. 'These times are very different from when you and I were young.'

'Think about it a little,' said Naresh, putting his hand on the phone's receiver to indicate that the meeting was over. 'I'm sure Mr Bhan can help my son.'

'Shall I serve lunch, Nareshji?' asked Pinki, getting up from her chair.

'Is it time already?'

'You are lost in your own world today, Nareshji,' said Pinki with a smile as she opened the clasp of her tiffin carrier and removed the boxes one at a time. Laying them out in a row, she brought out two square plastic containers from a drawer. These belonged to Naresh and Mr Asthana. Behind her desk, to one side, hidden by a large metal cupboard, was a small sink and a countertop on which sat a microwave oven – Mrs Asthana had bought it for the office. Pinki brought the plates to her table and arranged the food on them, adding vegetables from her own box to each one. She then loaded Mr Asthana's plate into the microwave, picked up her extension and warned him that his lunch was on the way. When the microwave beeped, she took the plate out, popped Naresh's plate in, put two large tablespoons of set yoghurt on Mr Asthana's plate and carried it into his chamber. Mr Asthana ate alone.

'How are the beans today?' asked Pinki when she returned.

'Very tasty,' said Naresh, tearing off a piece of chapatti and scooping up some more of the tasty beans with it. 'Bhabhi's potatoes are also very nice. Tangy. Just the way I like them.'

'Hmmm.'

'How is Bhabhi? Did she go to that shop in Sarojini Nagar?'

'Which shop?'

'Nareshji!' said Pinki, an affectionate exasperation playing on her face. 'You've forgotten already? That shop from where I bought that salwar kameez for Seema. Bhabhi liked it a lot. She said she wanted to go there. All this was discussed in front of you.'

'Yes, yes. Sarojini Nagar. She went. I think she went.'

'Did she buy anything?' asked Pinki, now convinced that Naresh had no idea what she was talking about.

'Yes. She bought some suits.'

'Let it be, Nareshji. Tell me what is bothering you.'

Naresh had got Pinki this job as additional assistant to Mr Asthana after her husband died in a car accident. Harkirat Singh and Naresh had joined the department at the same time, and even worked in the same section for the first few years. Naresh had liked Harkirat, a big man who delighted in telling dirty jokes, laughing louder than anyone else at his own jokes, his large stomach shaking uncontrollably as he laughed. Harkirat was also known to be incorruptible: the word was that he would fly into a rage if anyone tried to bribe him. Nonetheless, he didn't lose his affection for Naresh, even though Naresh's bribe-taking had only grown in scope since they had first met. Although he sometimes let on that he was aware of Naresh's reputation, Harkirat never chided him for following a path that was so different from his own.

When Harkirat's parents told him they had found a girl for him and that he should go and meet her, he had asked Naresh to accompany him to Pinki's parents' home. Naresh and Arti had attended Harkirat's wedding. They had waited outside the delivery room with Harkirat while Pinki gave birth to her son. And when the road accident claimed Harkirat, it had been Naresh who had made sure that everything that was due to Pinki from the department was given to her as quickly as possible, without her having to run from one section to another.

Harkirat's salary had been the only source of income for his household. His parents had died one after the other in the years following his marriage, their land in the village usurped by relatives whom Harkirat did not have the resources to fight in court. Pinki's father, too, had died and her mother lived with her. She had been a great source of comfort when Harkirat died, but when the fog of grief lifted, the old woman was yet another mouth that Pinki now had to feed.

Naresh stepped in. On evenings and weekends, he went to Pinki's house and coached her in shorthand. He studied old question papers of the stenographers' service entrance exam, deciphered the pattern and coached her intensively in each aspect of it. He got her the form for the exam and took her to the examination centre himself. When the results were about to be declared, he found out how Pinki had fared and, when he found that she had qualified, he called in a favour from a friend in the Ministry of Personnel to ensure that the candidates were allocated postings in such a way that Pinki came to his department. Once Pinki had joined the secretarial pool in his department, Naresh reminded Mr Asthana that someone of his seniority was entitled to a personal assistant and a stenographer. Once he had drafted the request and had it signed by Mr Asthana, it was easy for him to persuade the Establishment section to assign Pinki to the job.

'The children,' said Naresh. 'Both of them grown up and I still have to worry about them.'

'Is Seema okay?'

Naresh felt a rush of affection for this woman who knew him so well. She had remembered that he was worried about Praveen, they had talked it about it more than once. That's why when he had used the plural, children, she had asked about Seema.

'There's something wrong.'

'Did something happen at the wedding?'

'How do you know something happened at the wedding?'

'You told me you were going to the wedding. But you didn't mention it the next day. When you didn't say anything about the wedding, I thought maybe something happened there, but I said, leave it, if he wants to tell me, he will tell me.'

Her proportionate, finely featured face had a sympathetic expression on it. Above her slightly hooked nose, Naresh could see her eyes, trained downwards on her plate. The sight of her returning to her meal quietly, giving him the chance to speak without pushing him to talk, made him wonder for a moment why his wife could not be as undemanding and understanding. What a waste, he thought, that a woman who could read a man's moods so perfectly and soothe him with word and tone had no husband who could benefit from these qualities. 'I think her in-laws said something,' he said finally.

'It happens sometimes. His mother, the Guru keep her, was very strict with me in the early days.'

Suddenly, for the first time, Naresh felt a strong urge to tell Pinki about all the tests and treatments Seema had been through and the failure of the third round of in vitro fertilization. But he didn't. 'You're right. I hope it's nothing serious.'

'Nareshji, you worry too much. Besides, you yourself said, they are grown up. They have their own lives now. How long will you protect them from their destiny?'

'But it is my responsibility …'

'I know, Nareshji. It is every father's responsibility. But sometimes the right way to fulfil your responsibility is to relinquish it.'

'What nonsense,' said Naresh, irritated that a woman younger than him, whose own son was just twelve, was offering him this florid piece of advice. 'What do you know about relinquishing responsibility?'

Pinki's eyes widened. She blinked, then looked back at him. 'For many months,' she said when she finally spoke, each word emerging with some difficulty, 'the only responsibility I acknowledged was to my husband. And the only way I fulfilled that responsibility was by holding his photo to my chest and crying.'

'Pinki, I'm sorry,' said Naresh, reaching across the table with his hand, stopping just before it touched her shoulder.

'Then I relinquished that responsibility,' said Pinki.

2

A BLAST OF DAMP AIR HIT NARESH AS HE PUSHED OPEN THE door to his son-in-law's office. It was an oblong room, one-third the size of Mr Asthana's, a window at its far end half-blocked by a desert cooler that didn't appear to be cooling in any significant way. Behind a long desk at the far end of the room, his thick forearms beading with sweat, sat Ashok Sharma, Seema's husband, leaning over a file while a man sat across the desk watching him.

Naresh stepped in and cleared his throat. Ashok looked up and rose to his feet with an alacrity that pleased Naresh, shutting the file as he stood. His supplicant's face registered a look of dismay.

'Babuji,' said Ashok, walking out from behind his desk, 'how come you are here?'

'I just happened to be nearby,' said Naresh, stepping back as Ashok began bending slowly from his ample waist in a half-hearted attempt to touch his father-in-law's feet.

'No, no,' said Naresh, energetically lunging forward, his efforts preventing Ashok from reaching lower than knee level, 'there's no need for all this. I was nearby, so I thought I'd come and see you.'

The office of the Deputy Commissioner (East) lay along the eastern embankment of the river, in a part of the city that was distant and uninteresting for people who lived where Naresh lived – Central government housing in South Delhi, west of the river – and worked where Naresh worked, in the CGO complex on Lodhi Road in Central Delhi, also west of the river. But Ashok didn't question this improbable story and Naresh breathed a little easier.

'Any fool could guess he is your father,' said the man whose file had been shut. 'Your faces are so similar.'

'He is my father-in-law,' said Ashok, sitting heavily back down in his chair, indicating to Naresh that he should sit on the sofa that was placed between the door and the desk.

'Namaste, Sasurji,' said the man, favouring Naresh with an ingratiating smile.

'Let me just see this file, Babuji,' said Ashok, who had already picked the file up and was looking through it. 'Will you have some tea?'

While he waited for the tea to come and the file to be read, Naresh looked around the room. Its shape bothered him. In any government establishment, the important officers took the better rooms. Ashok Sharma, Naresh's son-in-law, was not minor in the scheme of things. This building housed the headquarters of the Deputy Commissioner of East Delhi, and Ashok was a sub-divisional magistrate. What a powerful position, people had said when the proposal had come for Seema. 'Great scope for extra income.' But now, in Ashok's oddly shaped office, for the first time, Naresh felt a little unsure of his son-in-law's status. Would he be able to get Praveen a job? What kind of job could he get him? And then, in a swirl of confusion, he remembered that asking Ashok to get Praveen a job had only been a pretext for coming here, not the real reason. The real reason had been Seema. She doesn't say anything, Arti had said, maybe you should go and talk to Ashokji and find out what is happening. Typical of her, he thought. She has the idea and I have to execute it. But then it wouldn't be appropriate for Arti to come to Ashok's office, nor could this conversation be had in Seema and Ashok's house. They couldn't even go there without being invited and, in the last few months, no invitations had been forthcoming. But still, thought Naresh, what can I find out from him? And what will I ask him?

'Your patwari has to certify the acquisition,' said Ashok, shutting the file. 'Without that we cannot do anything.'

'But Sharmaji,' said the supplicant, pointing to the file in a gesture intended, subliminally perhaps, to persuade Ashok to reopen it, 'this is for educational purposes. The patwari's certification is not needed.'

'Hmmm,' said Ashok, drawing circles around the maker's name on top of the file with his index finger. 'Then wait for a bit. This will take time.'

He rose from his desk and came and sat on the sofa next to Naresh. 'Is the tea okay?' he asked.

'Very nice,' said Naresh, although there was too much sugar in it.

'Everyone at home is fine, Babuji?' asked Ashok, picking up his own cup of tea.

Naresh glanced over at Ashok's desk. The man there was watching the two of them, his eyes focused on the cup of tea in Naresh's hand. 'I need your help, Ashokji,' said Naresh.

'Of course, of course, what can I do for you?' asked Ashok in a tone so friendly and warm that his supplicant's bemused eyes bounced up from the tea to his face.

'That, umm, er,' said Naresh, indicating with his eyes that he wasn't comfortable speaking with another person in the room.

'Please,' said Ashok. 'Don't worry. Speak freely.'

'Your brother-in-law,' began Naresh, reluctantly. 'Praveen.'

'How is he?' asked Ashok. 'I didn't see him at the wedding. Hadn't he come?'

'None of us saw you,' said Naresh, smiling to take the edge off the complaint.

'Sorry Babuji,' said Ashok. 'You know how many things need to be taken care of at a wedding. I scolded Seema later. I told her, I was busy, that's okay, but not so busy that I cannot meet my wife's family for two minutes.'

'The arrangements were very good,' said Naresh.

'Did Mummyji enjoy the chaat?' asked Ashok. 'We had it specially ordered from Old Delhi.'

'From Bazaar Sita Ram?' asked the supplicant from across the room. 'No chaat in the world is as good as theirs.'

'She enjoyed it very much,' said Naresh. 'She is very worried about Praveen. He stays out all night at the call centre, sleeps all day. He earns okay, but who knows what kind of company he keeps and what he does all night. We are both very worried.'

'Babuji,' said Ashok, smiling, 'all over India, people his age are doing these jobs. It's nothing to worry about.'

'My son also wanted to join a call centre,' said the supplicant. 'But I told him that while I was alive I wouldn't let him spoil his health. Besides, we all know what goes on in these places at night, all these boys and girls together.'

'You are absolutely right,' said Naresh, glad to have found an ally, but somewhat concerned at the prospect of the conversation veering into a general discussion on the moral decline of Indian youth. 'I should have also prohibited him. But his mother didn't let me.'

'A mother's heart, Sasurji,' said the supplicant, his voice strengthening with the legitimacy that Naresh's response had provided him. 'We men love our children like we love no one else, but we are always laid low by the power of a mother's heart.'

'Babuji,' said Ashok, cutting in. 'You know that I tried to guide him. But he wouldn't listen.'

'I know you did, Ashokji,' said Naresh, nodding vigorously.

'Ashokji is a very helpful person,' the supplicant said. 'Everyone says that if there is one person in this office who helps people, it is Ashokji.'

'I tried to tell him,' continued Ashok, 'that he needs to get some proper qualifications and look for a job that has some prospects. But he wouldn't listen. You know what his qualifications are.'

'BA, second division,' said Naresh.

'Exactly,' said Ashok, pursing his lips. 'It's difficult. I told him, do something else along with your BA, do some computer course or something like that. But he wouldn't listen.'

'No, but at the call centre they work with computers all the time.'

'It's difficult,' Ashok repeated.

'It is difficult, Ashokji,' said Naresh. 'Being a father is very difficult. After so many years I still have to worry about my children. At my age, I have to go from office to office trying to find my grown son a job.'

'Being a father is truly very difficult, Sasurji,' said the supplicant dolefully. 'Ashokji is young. His children, your grandchildren, are probably still in school. He will not understand the pain you and I share.'

'I have no children,' said Ashok, a strained note entering his voice.

'No children yet?' asked the supplicant. 'How long have you been married?'

'Three years,' replied Ashok, realizing immediately after he had spoken that he did not owe his supplicant an answer.

'Three years and no children,' said the man. 'Is there some problem?'

'There is no problem,' said Naresh hastily. 'No problem.'

'I know one Baba in Ghaziabad,' said the supplicant. 'He is a very holy man. He gives a powder. Mix it in milk and drink it twice a day. You are guaranteed to have children within three months.'

'You keep out of it,' Ashok snapped.

'No, no, Ashokji, I was just saying it for your benefit. This Baba has truly miraculous powers. At least visit him once.'

'Please, you ...' said Naresh.

Ashok raised his hand and silenced his father-in-law. His face was grim now. 'Please take your file and go,' he said, putting on his officer expression and looking straight into his supplicant's eyes. 'Come back next Tuesday.'

'Ashokji, I didn't mean to ...' said the supplicant, dismay taking over the querulous curiosity that had earlier animated his face.

Ashok looked away from him, indicating the door with his right hand.

The supplicant looked contrite at first, then defeated. He picked up his file from the desk. Then, turning back towards the sofas, he folded his hands, first towards Naresh and then towards Ashok. 'I'll go,' he said.

'Hmmm,' said Ashok, picking up his cup of tea and nursing it with both hands.

Naresh watched the door swing shut behind the departing man and wondered what he should say now.

'Okay, that's enough,' said Naresh. 'Tell me what the problem is.'

'No, Nareshji,' said Pinki, breaking open her samosa, clearing out the filling from it and bringing the crisp brown crust to her mouth. 'There's no problem.'

'How many years have I known you, Pinki?' asked Naresh.

'Some fourteen or fifteen years.'

'Now tell me,' said Naresh. 'What is the problem?'

They sat at one end of a long metal table, one of several that had been placed in this big hall that served as a canteen for the entire building. It was just past three in the afternoon and the canteen had only two patrons, Pinki and Naresh. A sweeper lay at full stretch on one side, fast asleep. The serving counter that was built into one of the walls had no one behind it – Naresh had waited a full minute before someone in the kitchen noticed him. The room's poor acoustics amplified and distorted the sound of the rickety ceiling fans that were blowing hot air down on empty tables. Their clatter created an envelope of noise whose centre, oddly enough, felt still and soothing.

'Is there a problem with Arjan's homework again?' Naresh asked.

Pinki's son Arjan had always been a shy little boy, and since his father had died he had become even quieter than he used to be. There had been a period when his teachers would send notes home saying that he wasn't doing his homework. His homework notebook had page after page with the homework question written at the top and squiggly lines below. He never fights with the other boys or talks in class, they would say, he is such a nice boy, it's only this homework, someone needs to take care of it. But Pinki was too tired to spend time with him after she got home from work and finished cooking, and her mother, who doted on the child, was just about able to read.

'No,' she said. 'It's the Guru's benevolence, Arjan is doing his homework.'

'Mummy's knees are bothering her again?'

'A little bit,' said Pinki. 'But ever since she started following Baba Ramdev's exercises in front of the TV every morning, the pain is in control.'

Naresh had one conjecture left. It was a conjecture that was painful for him to even formulate in his head, painful because it brought back the memory of his dead friend – a joke told, a meal shared, some quiet moments spent together, small shards of memory that punctured him in a hundred places. It was painful because he knew that this woman he cared so much for felt its pain every single day, he had seen it in her eyes every single day. So he said nothing. He kept looking at her face. Her brow was not creased, but her lips drooped at the corners and her eyes remained fixed on her cup of tea for what appeared to Naresh to be a very long time.

'Kamaljeet wrote Mummy a letter,' she said finally.

Kamaljeet was Pinki's brother-in-law, Harkirat's first cousin. A month after Pinki and Harkirat were married, Kamaljeet had come to Delhi and lived with them while he looked for a job and applied for emigration to Canada. He had stayed with them for almost a year before his immigration papers had come through; a year in which Pinki cooked for him, made him take her shopping and play cards with her and watch TV with her. Naresh had met him at that time and had liked him instantly. He was an energetic and respectful young man, who clearly adored Harkirat and loved Pinki like a sister. When Harkirat died Kamaljeet had been ready to jump on to a plane in Vancouver, where he drove a taxi, and come to Delhi, but Pinki forbade him. The first time you return home, she had said, it should be for happiness, not grief. Since that time, he had been writing to Pinki once a month and wired money every three months. Pinki never asked him for anything, and often wrote saying she didn't need the money and that he should save it for his wedding. But no matter what she said, the money would arrive with every third letter.

'But he writes every month,' said Naresh.

'He writes to me every month,' said Pinki. 'This time he wrote to Mummy.'

'What did he say?'

'He said he wants to get married,' said Pinki.

'Married?' asked Naresh. 'But that's a good thing. It's about time he got married.'

'He wants to marry me.'

In his early letters, just after he left for Canada, Kamaljeet would sometimes write that he felt lonely and that he wanted to get married. Harkirat spread the word amongst his relatives and friends, and proposals started coming in. But Kamaljeet would take a long time to respond to each proposal, eventually saying that the girl appeared to be very nice and was good looking, but he was not interested in marrying her. Initially he would add that he wanted a girl just like his sister-in-law. It was one of those flirtatious things that younger brothers-in-law sometimes said. Harkirat and Pinki both found it amusing. Pinki would write to him joking that she was already taken and saying that he shouldn't be fussy, otherwise he would grow old all alone. After a couple of years, the marriage proposals stopped coming; the word had gone around that this boy was difficult to please. Kamaljeet stopped bringing it up, and Harkirat overruled Pinki when she told him to try and convince Kamaljeet to keep looking, saying: 'Let the boy live his life his way, there's plenty of time left to get married.'

'He said he wanted to marry you?' Naresh asked.

'Yes.'

'Just like that?' asked Naresh, making an effort to keep his voice even. 'I want to marry Pinki Bhabhi.'

'Yes,' she said. 'I have a lot of love and respect for her, he wrote. I want to marry her.'

Naresh felt his head tightening. His left thigh started shaking involuntarily. 'What did Mummy say?' he asked in the most even tone he could manage.

'She thinks it's a good idea,' Pinki said. 'He is such a caring boy. He will take good care of you, she says. And he loves Arjan like a son, always asks about him, sends gifts for him every year on his birthday.'

With a massive sigh, the entire ensemble of ceiling fans switched off. Silence filled the hall, punctuated by the sleeping sweeper's soft snores.

'Looks like the electricity has gone,' said Pinki. 'Let's hope it comes back soon.'

'And what did you say?' asked Naresh.

'About what?' asked Pinki.

'To Kamaljeet,' said Naresh. 'About marriage.'

'What can I say?' asked Pinki. 'There is nothing to say.'

She's going to marry him, Naresh thought. His inner voice started sounding in his head, speaking frantically. And why shouldn't she, it made a lot of sense. It was difficult for a woman to manage without a man, especially a woman who had to take care of a young child and an old mother. You yourself have often thought of telling her to get married. What is wrong if she marries Kamaljeet? With an effort he silenced the voice. Then he took a deep breath. 'So, are you going to marry him?' he asked.

'Nareshji, please,' said Pinki, fanning her face with her hand. 'The question does not arise. How can I?'

'Why?' asked Naresh reaching for his cup of tea. The relief that flooded through him made him crave the sensation of hot sweet tea running down his throat.

'I have given myself to one man, Nareshji,' said Pinki. 'I can't give myself to another.'

'Hmph,' said Naresh. 'That sounds like a dialogue from an old Hindi film.'

'Think whatever you want,' said Pinki, straightening her back. 'That's how I feel.'

'So you will never consider getting married, to anyone?' asked Naresh.

A group of men came into the canteen, chatting and laughing. One of them waved to Naresh. 'What news, Nareshji?' he asked loudly.

Naresh smiled at him and waved back, and then turned away so that the man didn't feel inclined to come up to him. 'The Accounts section has decided to have their tea here, now that the electricity is gone,' he said, bringing his cup to his lips and draining its contents. 'Let's go back now, Asthana Saheb's meeting will end soon.'

Pinki looked into her cup. It was more than half full. She took a sip, but the tea had gone cold. Putting the cup down, she rose slowly to her feet, picking up a small part of the potato filling of her samosa as she stood. 'Who has seen tomorrow, Nareshji,' she said as they walked back to their office, 'but today I know that if even the Guru himself appeared before me and told me to marry someone, I would refuse.'

On their honeymoon, Ashok and Seema had decided to postpone having children for a couple of years. 'Let us enjoy each other's company for a while,' Ashok had said. Arti had protested when Seema told her about the plan. 'They will think you're shameless. Your mother-in-law will think you are teaching him all this.'

But Seema was not worried. It was Ashok's idea, not hers, he would be the one to take the blame and, from her side, to get the credit for it. But in the spirit of her mother's advice, she registered a faint protest in front of her in-laws when Ashok told them. Her mother-in-law, Sarla, had grumbled at first, then agreed, and for almost a year after that, the question of children had not come up, except for gentle hints here and there. It had been a wonderful time for Seema. Ashok was clearly besotted with her looks and charmed by her vivacious personality. He would take her shopping to the Rajouri Garden malls, strutting through the air-conditioned arcades, showing off his new wife. He took her to see a movie every weekend.

They would eat at a different restaurant every time they went out. That summer they holidayed in the hills. That winter they went to Goa.

Early in the second winter of her married life, Seema went to Muzaffarnagar along with Ashok and his parents for a wedding on Ashok's father's side of the family. One evening, Seema had gone shopping with some of Ashok's younger cousins. The men were congregating for the evening's drink and the older ladies were organizing and reorganizing masses of new clothes and jewellery and gifts. Shobha Chachi, a distant relative, some kind of cousin sister-in-law to Sarla – but one who had been close to her several years earlier, when they had shared a house in Delhi for a while – started talking about how she knew of a holy man in a village just outside Mathura.

'He has helped many people,' she said, 'there is a lot of faith placed in him.'

At first Sarla had not understood, but then Shobha Chachi went on to talk about a fertility clinic in Delhi someone had told her about: 'You stay in Delhi, it must be close to your house.'

Sarla protested: 'The children want to wait a little while.'

But Shobha's expression, concern mixed with pity, made it obvious that she thought this was just a brave front. She went right on, talking about doctors and godmen and pilgrimages. When she started talking which of the two – Ashok or Seema – was to blame for the condition, Sarla felt anger rise in her, anger born of helplessness at the knowledge that the only way to convince people that nothing was wrong with her son or daughter-in-law was to show them a child. Shobha, she knew, spoke without malice. She was meddlesome but she was a well-wisher. If someone as sympathetic as her thought this way, what were other people thinking? What would they say? What were they saying?

That night, when Seema returned to the house, her mother-in-law was cold towards her for the very first time. Seema noticed, but didn't think much of it, the way the first symptoms of a disease are often disregarded. But on their return from Muzaffarnagar, she had to admit that Sarla's behaviour had changed. The next time Sarla talked about how she was waiting for a grandchild, there was nothing gentle about the suggestion. Someone must have said something to her at the wedding, Seema told Ashok. But there was nothing he could do to reverse what had happened. There was nothing either of them could do to take what had been said and make it unsaid. And so, in the months following the wedding, Ashok and Seema started trying to have a baby.

Sarla was overjoyed when her daughter-in-law told her they had started the process of giving her a grandchild. And at first, she was patient and supportive: 'It takes time, sometimes it can take many attempts.' But as one menstrual cycle after another came and went, Sarla's patience began to wear thin. Ashok began to worry as well. On carefully selected nights, he would make love mechanically, ensuring he came deep inside her, making her lie on her back with a pillow under her buttocks for half an hour afterwards. The trips to the mall and the movies became more and more infrequent, replaced now with trips to doctors and temples.

Ashok's semen was tested. It was fine. Seema's ovaries and her uterus were also in good shape. But when an ultrasound investigation was done, it was found that her eggs were not descending into her uterus. So the doctor suggested a hysterosalpingography. When the imaging results came, it was found that Seema's fallopian tubes were blocked. 'It can happen sometimes,' the doctor said, 'because of infection or because of genetic factors. And many times, it just clears up on its own. Try for some more time.'

On the way home from the gynaecologist, Ashok kept saying, it's okay, don't worry, we'll keep trying. But when they got home, he told Sarla about the problem with Seema's tubes. How could he not have told her? Seema would think whenever she thought back to that moment. After all, she had never asked him to keep any secret from his mother, she had never wanted that. He was just being honest. He explained everything. It may take some time, he had said. When he finished speaking, Sarla stood up. Our destiny was bad, she said, and gave Seema a look that made it clear that 'our' did not include her, that when Sarla said that their destiny was bad, she was talking about the happenstance that had brought Seema into their lives as Ashok's wife.

Some days afterwards, Ashok told Seema that he had asked around and he thought they should try in vitro fertilization. Seema knew from the way he said it, the way he avoided making eye contact with her when he said it, that the idea had come from his mother. More trips to doctors and clinics followed as did rounds of hormonal treatments that lasted weeks. Either the medicines or the fact that her mother-in-law had turned again and become extremely solicitous of her needs made Seema feel despair of the sort she had never felt before. She hid it as best as she could from everyone around her. 'Once the baby comes, it will be okay,' she kept telling herself. Finally the eggs were extracted and fertilized. And a few days later, the first round of implantation was done.

For three weeks they waited. In those three weeks, Sarla fussed over her daughter-in-law like she had never fussed over her before: not letting her do any work around the house, cooking all her favourite food. Then the result of the pregnancy test came and Seema's second honeymoon ended.

Naresh had been feeling restless since evening. Khanna had taken Arti and him to show them a shopping complex that the Bhan Group was building in a new sector of Gurgaon. The deal was that the Bhan Group would lease one shop in this complex to Praveen for a period of ten years and organize a soft loan for him to start a business there. Pointing out tall luxury developments and big individual houses that were coming up around the location where the Bhan Group was constructing, Khanna had said: 'Your son can sell bread and eggs here and make money. Any business will flourish in this location. With a little effort, he can make more money in a year than you have earned in the last twenty years.'

Arti had been so pleased with the arrangement that when they returned, she had gone to the market herself and bought Naresh the oily kachoris he loved dearly, the ones the doctor had forbidden him to eat. She had heated two for him and when he had looked up from the plate, he had seen her gaze at him with pride. His taste buds were thanking her as he ate, but somewhere deeper, there was something that felt like anger, some dissatisfaction, something nebulous and acrid that was clearly directed at his wife. More than twelve hours had passed since then. It was three-thirty in the morning and the unease had not left. He tossed and turned in bed for a while, then gave up, got up and went to the kitchen.

He put the milk in with the tea leaves, boiling them together. A few years ago, Arti had decided that she wanted to drink tea the fancy way, draining the tea leaves away, then adding a bit of milk when the liquid had been poured into the cup. Naresh had gone along with it – not that he had an option. But he missed the strong taste of boiled tea, and he suspected that Arti missed it too, because occasionally, when they were away from home and she had to drink tea the old way, he could see that she savoured it with artless spontaneity. Alone in the kitchen, late at night, Naresh waited for the tea to boil to a satisfactory darkness before taking it off the stove and pouring it into a cup. Carrying the cup with him, he walked out to the balcony and stood there with his thighs rubbing against the balustrade.

Naresh lived in what the government called quarters. Each building had two storeys, each storey had two flats whose doors faced each other – making it impossible for their occupants to ignore each other. Each such building was placed against the next, forming an unbroken wall of flats a few hundred feet wide that stood facing its twin across an area that once had grass growing on it and was still referred to as the lawns, but was now mostly dust with a few scattered clumps of green. In the upper-storey flats – Naresh and Arti lived in one – there was a small veranda at the front of the house. Most people had put a wooden framework of windows to make a small room out of that veranda, but, despite the urgings of his neighbours, Naresh had decided against it. He liked to stand out on the veranda sometimes in the evenings with his tea, maybe wave a greeting at someone taking a walk, or just watch the colony's boys playing cricket on the lawns. Standing in that balcony, he had seen cycles being replaced with scooters and scooters being replaced with cars. He had seen babies start walking and schoolgirls become brides. But this place was not like the place Naresh had grown up in, where the entire cycle of human life was lived out in one place. Here you saw people for a while before they moved on, and maybe, if you were lucky, you saw them go from one stage of their lives to the next.

Families lived here for several years at a time – Naresh and Arti had been in their apartment for almost eight years now – but no matter how long they stayed, there was always a near or distant future looming ahead of them, where they would have to return this house to the government, 'surrender it' as the phrase went, and move to some other place, leaving this house to new occupants. Some looked forward to that future with anticipation: they moved because they were promoted and became entitled to something bigger somewhere else, or if they were retiring, they were moving away from Delhi, back to whichever town or village they came from, or they were staying in Delhi but had managed, by fair or foul means, to organize themselves something spacious in a nice location that was well connected and where, most importantly, the property prices were on their way up. Some looked forward to that future with apprehension: they moved because they were being posted to some remote part of India, or they had retired and would now have to live in some small place far from the centre of Delhi, or in some house whose rent would be a real rent, not the nominal amount the government charged its employees. But however they felt about it, they all had to move. And when they moved, they left behind a layer of memories that, like the whitewash on the walls, would be scraped off and thrown away before the next occupants moved in.

Looking out onto the lawn that lay below his balcony, the first sips of tea warm in his stomach, Naresh's mind wandered back to the time when a tent had been put up on the lawn for Seema's wedding. He could see it clearly in his head: the caterers had put their stoves here, the tentwallah had positioned the generator there, workers had built the gateway just below his flat, then hoisted it up like they were raising the roof of a house. What busy, happy days those had been. Not a single expense had been spared. He might be an important official, Naresh had told his neighbours, but let him not think his father-in-law is a nobody. And Seema had looked so beautiful in her red sari, covered in gold. He had wept when she got into the flower-bedecked car and left. She had become an adult, a woman, that little baby bubbling at the mouth when the nurse handed her to him in the hospital. She had been a sickly child, prone to illness in her early years. He had always taken her to the best doctors he could afford, bought her medicines from private shops, rather than taking them from the government dispensary where they sometimes sold the good medicines on the black market and passed off expired tablets and adulterated powders to legitimate patients. He had always taken care of her the way a father should, throwing the net far and wide to find her the best possible groom. He had married her to a sub-divisional magistrate, what more could a father do? He had delivered her to a family he had thought would take care of her for the rest of her life. And now, this twist of fate, this constriction in her destiny that didn't allow her to have children. What could he do about it? Maybe she had not seen the right doctor, Naresh thought. He knew someone in AIIMS, a section officer called Bhutani he had once helped with some property matter. He would talk to Bhutani. The doctors at AIIMS were the best in India, surely one of them could help her. But would her husband like it if he intervened? Would his pride not be hurt? I'll talk to Arti about this tomorrow morning, Naresh thought. We are her parents after all; if we don't help her, who will? Yes, I'll call Bhutani tomorrow itself, no matter what Arti says. I'll ask him to get us an appointment with the best doctor in AIIMS.

Feeling better at the thought of talking to Bhutani, he raised his cup to his mouth and found his tea had gone cold. As he turned to take the cup back to the kitchen, the sound of a motorcycle engine broke the night's silence. Naresh looked down and saw a single headlight coming up the asphalt path. The motorcycle came and stopped right below Naresh's balcony.

Praveen switched the engine off and swung his right leg off the bike. From the balcony above, his father watched him take his helmet off and tuck it under his arm. Praveen ran his hand through his hair, then straightened his shirt and walked into the building. Why doesn't he tuck his shirt into his pants? thought Naresh, turning to go into the house.

'You're home, Beta,' said Naresh, opening the front door.

Praveen looked up with a start. 'I have my keys,' he said, his hand coming out of his pocket with the keys in them. 'You didn't have to get up.'

'I was awake. I saw you come, so I opened the door.'

'Oh,' said Praveen, putting his keys back into his pocket. 'That's okay.'

'What time is it?' Naresh asked.

'Must be around four,' said Praveen.

'Is this the time you normally come home?'

'Maybe you can interrogate me after I come in,' said Praveen.

'Sorry,' said Naresh, taking half a step back. Praveen's helmet got stuck on the doorpost when he tried to enter through the narrow space left by Naresh. He twisted forward to release it, brushing against his father as it came loose. A sharp odour hit Naresh's nose. It was a familiar smell, something he had smelt earlier, not once but many times. Where had he come across it before? Praveen was already past him and walking towards the kitchen when Naresh realized with a shock that the boy smelt of sex.

'Oh Mummy,' said Seema, rolling her eyes, 'these don't match. Even Minu wouldn't want to wear this combination.'

'Who is Minu?' asked Arti, tilting her head sideways to examine once again the sari and blouse she had been holding up to show her daughter. Her previously held conviction that they matched perfectly was now wavering.

'You've forgotten Minu? The newsreader on Doordarshan. Remember how her blouses were always one shade wrong for her saris?'

Arti giggled. 'Yes, of course,' she said. 'You remember after all this time. That was so long ago.'

'Who can forget such a thing, Mummy?' said Seema. 'Every time she came on the news, you would say the same thing: who sells her these blouses?'

'Actually,' cut in the older balding man, who had been listening to their conversation from behind the counter with a patience that only shopkeepers possess, 'Minuji buys her blouse material from our shop. She has been coming here for more than twenty-five years.'

'Oh,' said Seema, hiding a smile with her hand.

'Why don't you tell her the problem?' asked Arti. 'The whole of India knows her blouses don't match.'

'We can only suggest,' said the man. 'The final decision is always the customer's.'

'That may be,' said Arti, who now sounded genuinely aggrieved, 'but you also have a duty.'

'Your daughter is right,' said the man, almost snatching the blouse material from Arti. 'This does not match. I'll show you the right shade.'

When they came out of the shop, Seema linked her arm in her mother's. 'Good you scolded him, Mummy,' she said. 'He can't escape the blame so easily.'

'Are you making fun of me?' asked Arti.

'No, Mummy,' said Seema. 'Not at all.'

Arti stopped and turned to her daughter. Disregarding the morning shoppers walking by, she took Seema's chin between her index finger and thumb. 'It's good to see you smiling,' she said.

At Jain Sari Centre, they looked at the new stock of cotton saris that had come in the previous week. The salesman, sitting with his legs folded under him, tirelessly unfolded one sari after another, creating two piles when they were handed back to him: not interested and maybe. A helper, perhaps an apprentice, carefully folded the saris from the not interested pile and stacked them neatly to one side.

'Show me that one,' said Arti, pointing to a beige Maheshwari on the shelf behind the salesman.

'It's beautiful, Mummy,' said Seema when the sari was unfolded, its intricate pattern of small motifs in gold thread revealed. 'Look at this work.'

'You know who would really like this one?' said Arti. 'Sarlaji.'

'That's right,' said Seema, the delight leaching out of her

voice at the mention of her mother-in-law's name. 'But she already has so many saris.'

After a satisfactory session at Jain, they moved on to La Mode, where the tailor master greeted them with a shifty smile that signified that he had, as usual, not completed the work they had given him the last time they were here. Seema took out a blouse from her bag and showed him where it pinched her arm. 'You do this every time, Masterji,' said Arti, like she said every time. He took the faultily tailored blouse and marked it with chalk in a few places, like he did every time, and tossed it to one side. Arti took out the blouse pieces she had just bought and dumped them on the counter: 'Here,' she said. 'When will you get them done? And this time, tell me when you will really be done. Do you know how far we have to travel to get our blouses tailored at your shop?'

Finally, at lunch in Bengali Market, waiting for their food to arrive, Seema said: 'Babuji had gone to his office the other day.'

'Yes, Beta, he had.'

'Why?'

'You know we are worried about Praveen. I was the one who suggested it to your father. I told him, Ashokji has such an important post, maybe he can find his brother-in-law a job.'

'What did Ashokji say?'

'He didn't say anything. Did he say something to you?'

'No.'

'He doesn't talk to you about these things?'

'Mummy!' said Seema, annoyed by her mother's prying.

'You should ask him to help your brother,' said Arti, unfazed.

'Mummy, are you worried about Praveen or are you worried about your daughter?'

It took Arti a moment to recover from the directness of the question. 'Beta, you know I am worried about you,' she said finally. 'You haven't told me what happened, but when I saw your face that day at the wedding, I knew that something had happened. I know the third round failed, but you were so confident when the treatment started and Ashokji was also so supportive. If this doesn't work, we will do something else, he said, and if nothing works, we will adopt a child. Then what happened?'

The waiter brought a tray to their table and unloaded two plates on to it. Seema looked at the slurry of chhole that lay on her plate and the two swollen bhaturas that sat alongside, steam rising from them, golden brown pimples on their surface still sizzling with remnants of hot oil. She pushed the plate to one side. 'He brought the report home the day before the wedding,' she said, 'the pregnancy test report after the third round. Mummyji was also there. When he came in and put the envelope down, she took one look at his face, then turned to me and said, I want a grandson that is my own flesh and blood. If you can't give me one, I will find a girl who can.'

'She said that!' Arti gasped. Her hand, raised to tear a piece of bhatura, fell back on the table.

'Yes. Then she walked out of the room.'

'How dare she say such a thing!' Arti's voice rose. An older man sitting at the next table turned to look at them.

'Shh, Mummy.'

'Who does she think she is?' said Arti, anger pouring out of her now lowered voice.

'I picked up the envelope and opened it,' said Seema, the memory of that futile action finally bringing tears to her eyes. 'Maybe, I thought, just maybe he hadn't read the report right. Maybe I was actually pregnant.'

It was not a minute past nine-thirty in the morning on Naresh's watch when the phone rang.

'Has Asthana Saheb arrived?' said the voice on the other end. 'Minister Saheb wants to talk to him.' It was Bhushanji, personal assistant to the minister.

'He just arrived,' said Naresh, wondering why Bhushanji had not greeted him or asked him what the latest news was.

'Put him on the line,' said Bhushanji. 'Minister Saheb is waiting.' His tone – aloof, formal – sent a flutter through Naresh's stomach.

'I'll connect him.'

'And Naresh,' said Bhushanji, dropping the 'ji' from Naresh's name, the ji that had always been optional –

Bhushanji was much older than Naresh and in a much more powerful position – but had, nevertheless, always been in evidence, 'this is a personal call. Disconnect your line.'

The red light on Naresh's phone remained lit for almost ten minutes and, for those ten minutes, Naresh's eyes were glued to it. Finally it went off, its imprint slowly fading from his retina. He wished it hadn't gone off. Bhushanji's voice held a presentiment of something that would not arrive while the light was on. But it had gone off now and, whatever the news was, he would have to face it. His eyes were still on that extinguished red light when the phone rang, a loud, harsh ring, one that he heard every day, a ring that grated on his ears today and made his head throb.

'Naresh,' said Mr Asthana. 'Come in here.'

The air-conditioner in Mr Asthana's room was operating at full blast but his high forehead was beaded with sweat. He was loosening the knot of his tie when Naresh entered the room. The jacket of his suit was draped over his chair. A strand of hair had fallen onto his forehead. It was the first time in all the years that Naresh had known him that Mr Asthana's hair wasn't groomed, not combed over neatly to one side.

'Minister Saheb had called,' Mr Asthana said.

'Yes, sir,' Naresh replied.

'There is a problem.'

'What happened, sir?'

'He has received an anonymous complaint about the Port Trust deal,' Mr Asthana said.

'But, sir, that was closed almost three years ago,' said Naresh. He remembered the Port Trust deal very well. The money he had made on it had paid for Seema's wedding. It had been done quite smoothly, he just had to tell the winning bidder which caterer to pay and which tentwallah. Their people had also bought jewellery and saris for Ashok's family and a car for Ashok. Mr Asthana had also done very well off that deal: discounted stock in a company that was yet to go public, a laptop, a free vacation to the USA for his wife and daughter.

'I know,' said Mr Asthana, getting up from his chair and reaching for the water jug that sat on a sideboard. 'He said he is ordering a departmental inquiry.'

'Inquiry?'

'Yes,' said Mr Asthana, pouring water into a glass, then touching his forehead with the glass before drinking the water. 'Inquiry. We have to act fast. All the papers of the Port Trust deal have to be checked. Remove the ones they shouldn't see.'

'But Asthana Saheb,' said Naresh, 'the Port Trust deal was closed almost three years ago.'

'Are you going to keep repeating the same thing like a broken record?' snapped Mr Asthana, putting the glass down on the sideboard with a thud and turning to face Naresh. 'Nareshji, you are too old a player to not recognize the game. Don't you see what's happening?'

'What's happening, sir?'

'The Vijay Group has bought the minister,' said Mr Asthana, returning to his seat. 'They know I will never let them win this bid. So they went over my head and bought the minister. And he says anonymous complaint. Hmph! He thinks I was born yesterday.'

'If there is a departmental inquiry ...'

'I will be suspended,' said Mr Asthana, leaning back in his chair now. 'They will have to assign this deal to someone else while the inquiry is on. That someone else will kick the Bhan Group out of the bidding in the easiest possible way, saying that their bid is too expensive. The environmental sub-committee's report will remain suppressed and the Vijay Group will win the bid.'

Naresh felt dizzy. He leant on a chair for support, then gingerly went around and sat down on it.

'Why are you sitting down, Nareshji?' asked Mr Asthana, bringing his chair forward with a jerk. 'We don't have time. Not just the Port Trust deal, we have to scan the papers of all the deals that we have done in the eight years we have been in this department. If they can reopen the Port Trust papers, they can reopen anything. And all the new papers, the property papers, where are they?'

'In my safe outside,' said Naresh, pointing weakly to the door.

'You have lost your mind, Naresh,' said Mr Asthana, his voice rising. 'That's the first place they will look. Go and remove them immediately.'

'But, sir,' said Naresh, rising from the chair, still holding on to it for support. 'How has all this happened so suddenly?'

'It's partly my fault and partly your fault. My fault because I didn't tell Mr Bhan to ensure that this greedy bastard minister is paid off, and your fault because you didn't even know that the Vijay Group had approached him and bought him. Where has your head been all these days, Nareshji?'

'Sorry, sir.'

'I thought you were a capable person,' said Mr Asthana. His anger having found a focus, he regained his earlier self-possession. 'But I see now that you are an idiot.'

'But, sir,' said Naresh, stung by the insult, 'for the last eleven years I have worked for you. I have never given you any reason to complain. You brought me here to this department with you, you specially had me transferred here.'

It was true, thought Asthana, he had been both loyal and competent all these years. He looked at Naresh, standing in front of him, eyes averted, a hurt expression on his face. 'Okay, let that go now,' he said, pushing his tie's knot back into place, the apology in his tone rather than the words. 'We don't know how much time we have and there is a lot of work to do.'

'Sir,' said Naresh, emboldened, 'my family's future is in your hands.'

'Stop your drama, Nareshji,' said Mr Asthana, trying to scotch this line of conversation. 'Think of what needs to be done.'

'What can we do now, sir?'

'First let us clean up our papers,' said Mr Asthana, walking over to a large metal cupboard that stood to one side. 'Then let me make a few phone calls. It's just a departmental inquiry so far, he hasn't asked the CBI to investigate. Or if he has, he didn't tell me he has.'

'Can you manage the departmental inquiry, sir?'

'Maybe,' said Mr Asthana. He had opened the cupboard and was taking stacks of files out and throwing them on the floor. 'Help me, Nareshji.'

Naresh went over and started removing files from the cupboard. A knock on the door made him turn.

'Sir,' Pinki's voice came from the other side of the door. 'Can I come in?'

Before Mr Asthana could answer, the door swung open and Pinki came in. She was holding two sheets of paper in her hand. 'Sir, these just came from the Establishment Section.'

Mr Asthana took the papers from Pinki. He read through the first sheet, grimaced slightly, then looked at the second. 'Here, Nareshji,' he said, handing the second sheet of paper to Naresh without turning to face him. 'You have been suspended from your job with immediate effect.'

3

THE FIRST FEW DAYS AFTER THE SUSPENSION ORDER CAME, Naresh felt like he was on holiday. Arti's constant exhortations – do something about this, go and talk to someone, use your contacts to get out of this mess – heightened that vacation feeling. It made him feel like a truant schoolboy who had magically acquired immunity from his mother's importuning. He heard out what she said, nodded along, promised he would do whatever she wanted him to do, then returned to the newspaper. Leaning back into the extra time that had suddenly become available, he felt the accumulated stress of the everyday dissolving. The morning's race to get ready on time had disappeared, as had the daily ordeal through rush-hour traffic. He spent those first days luxuriating in the absence of a routine, enjoying the quiet outside his windows during the day, a weekday quiet more perfect than any he had experienced on a weekend. Occasionally he did try to worry about what had happened, or focus on finding a way out, but in those first few days of release, it was as if some mysterious unguent salved all anxiety. Then Arti tired of being ignored and stopped saying anything, and the feeling of freedom went as inexplicably as it had come.

In the past, when Naresh stayed home on a working day, it was because of illness or because a relative was visiting or when Seema's wedding was imminent. Those were exceptional situations – either debilitating or busy or joyous – and the house wrapped itself around them, becoming a nursing home or a hotel or the command centre of a complex operation. But this time, there were no special circumstances. And so, Naresh had to witness the weekday rhythms of his house as they really were.

The sweeper woman came at nine. She went room by room, first with her broom, then with a bucket of water and her swab. When she came through the living room, he would try and lift his legs to get out of her way, then, finding that uncomfortable, he would go to his room and continue reading the paper there, only to find her coming in there next. He tried telling Arti once or twice to get the sweeper to skip the living room, but she refused: 'Do you know how much dust comes in here? She should be cleaning twice a day.'

By eleven, the sweeper woman would be done and Arti would also have finished cleaning the kitchen after the morning's cooking. She would take the clothes out of the washing machine – it had been Naresh's gift to her on their twentieth anniversary – and put them out to dry. By this time, Naresh would be done with the newspaper and Arti would have gone in for her bath. After her bath, for a few days in the beginning, she sat with him for a while, but when the topic turned to his suspension, he would pick up the newspaper. So she resumed her normal activities – either sitting down with one of her magazines or going over to a neighbour's house to exchange gossip.

Arti ate lunch at one-thirty, then watched soap operas on TV for an hour before taking an hour's nap. These two hours were the most difficult of the day for Naresh. He disliked soap operas. 'Real people don't behave like this,' he would say. But to Arti's rejoinder, 'Then why not just treat it like fantasy,' he had no reply.

Earlier, when he went to the office, he would have to contend with only one hour of this kind of television in the evening, managing to tolerate it by hiding behind the newspaper or going out for a walk, ensuring that the TV was switched to the news at nine. But now, with the newspaper finished before lunch and the sun beating down outside, there was no way to avoid the television except to go into the bedroom and lie down. But the sound effects and shrill dialogues of the soaps leaked in through the gaps between the door and the wall, and sleep eluded him.

He would be exhausted and restless by the time Arti came in for her nap, but he would pretend to be asleep till her breathing grew even. Then he would open his eyes and stare at the ceiling fan till it was time to get up.

Arti woke up around four and went into the kitchen. Praveen would also get up around then, so she would make him a heavy snack and make herself some tea. Now that Naresh was home, he sat with them at teatime, but found that Praveen was usually groggy and Arti, evidently habituated to her son's uncommunicative behaviour, read a magazine as she sipped her tea. Sitting quietly at the table, Naresh would find himself waiting for 6 p.m. That was the time he returned from office, the time after which this house that he had plotted and pleaded and sweated to have allotted to him, this house where every single object, durable and consumable, had been bought with the money he had earned, this house where every single person ate because he worked, this house that didn't seem to possess the generosity to keep him during the day, this same house would open up and welcome him back. Shamelessly ignoring the fact that he had not left all day, the house would readmit him into its rigid routine.

Watching this routine unfold in front of him from one day to the next, Naresh felt not just excluded but cheated. Arti's day alternated between physically demanding chores – cooking, cleaning – and rest. When she worked, she was fully involved in what she did, satisfaction evident on her face when she finished. When she watched TV, she watched it with wholehearted engagement, entering into the stories she was told, snapping out of it the moment the credits rolled. And when it was time for rest, it was the rest of the deserving: when she lay down, she slept. In contrast, he spent his days in the office in a semi-alert state, waiting for work that was neither physically nor emotionally demanding. That constant tension, from nine in the morning to five-thirty in the evening, was why his hair was falling, he thought. It was why he had no energy for anything, why his stomach was always in some kind of trouble, why he couldn't sleep at night. More than twenty years of waiting at half-stretch had worn him out. Anger and self-pity filled him when he thought of this. And that anger, finding no other target, turned on Arti. He chafed at the unfairness of the situation, feeling stupid that in the early years of their marriage he had felt sorry for her, shut in as she was all day. He had thought that he was lucky to be able to go out into the world, attributing his better lot to his primary good fortune of having been born a man. How could he not have seen that her life, her honest, hardworking life, was so much better than what he had to endure? And now, in this difficult time, why could she not be more sympathetic, more accommodating? Why could she not see that everything he had been through all these years had been endured so that her comforts could be ensured and her family looked after? Why did she not understand that everything he had done in these two decades, right and wrong, he had done so that her life could play out its restful rhythms undisturbed?

But then, he would think, he was, after all, a man. A man's duty was to go out and work in the world and provide for his family. He could not fashion a routine like the one she had. Being a man, he did not even want his life to be like hers. His routine, his daily endeavour, came to him with his job and, good or bad, it was his own to live out in whatever way he could. He would begin to think of the power and prestige he enjoyed as a man, the things he could do that women could not do. But, as he thought through this and reached for the feeling of contentment that he had once known, the power he had as a man would begin to feel like nothing more than a corollary of the power he had known as Mr Asthana's assistant. All his other attributes would begin to fade in importance and the enormity of what suspension from his job meant would begin to loom. This is a temporary thing, he would say to himself. But his mind would not let him stop there. It would go on: if the inquiry committee found him guilty and recommended his dismissal, then this temporary loss would become permanent. This indefinite sentence – he had begun to think of it as house arrest – would then have a definite term, a term that would end only when his life itself ended.

'Pinki! No phone, nothing, and you're here,' said Arti, holding the door open, the delight evident in her voice. 'How come?'

'Sorry, Bhabhi,' said Pinki. 'Every time I ask your husband if I can come, he makes some excuse or the other, so I just came without telling him or you.'

'Good,' said Arti, embracing her. 'Maybe you can pull him out of his bad mood.'

'Where is he?'

'He's lying down,' said Arti, pursing her lips.

'At this time?' Pinki looked at her watch; it was almost six in the evening.

'You tell him. He doesn't listen to me.'

Pinki nodded. Arti waved her to the sofa.

'This sofa is very nice, Bhabhi,' said Pinki, running her hand over the wooden armrest.

'It's from a shop in Ghitorni,' said Arti. 'On the way to Gurgaon.'

'How much did it cost?'

'If I tell you, your bhaisaheb will be very angry,' said Arti. Then lowering her voice to a whisper, she said, 'Thirty thousand.'

Pinki looked shocked for a moment. 'It's very nice,' she said, her face falling into what she intended to be a look of admiration, but could easily have been mistaken for appalled disapproval.

When Naresh emerged from his bedroom – his shirt creased from having been slept in – Pinki noted with some relief that at least he appeared to have shaved recently.

'You didn't have to come,' said Naresh, but his voice betrayed his words. It was good to see Pinki.

'How are you, Nareshji?'

'Like you see me. Will you have some tea?'

Pinki talked, at first, about how she now had no work in the office. Mr Asthana's files were all being sent to the minister's office directly. Bhushanji checked in with her every other day, just in case some paper had come to her instead of him, but not one had, not even by mistake. She spent her days reading magazines and playing Solitaire on the office computer. The first few days, she took her boxes to the canteen at lunchtime. But whichever table she went to, people would grow silent suddenly when they saw her coming, so she stopped going.

'They look at each other and smirk when they think I'm not looking,' said Pinki. 'Sometimes I feel like slapping them.'

'They enjoy another person's misfortune,' said Arti. 'Those same people would come wagging their tails to him when they needed something.'

'Leave it,' said Naresh brusquely. 'Let's talk about something else.'

They sat in silence for a while, Pinki looking into her teacup, Arti at Naresh and Naresh at the wall behind Pinki's head.

'How is Aunty?' Arti asked, finally.

'Mummy has only one thing on her mind nowadays,' said Pinki, her voice brightening with relief at this conversational gambit.

'That marriage thing,' said Arti.

'Nareshji told you?' asked Pinki, glancing over at Naresh.

'It's only in the last few weeks that he has gone silent,' said Arti, sighing. 'Earlier he would tell me everything.'

'I haven't gone silent,' said Naresh. Both women turned to look at him, but he had nothing further to say.

'Anyway, so, what is Aunty saying?'

'The same thing. He is a good boy. He will take care of you.'

'But you don't want to ...'

'I don't know, Bhabhi. I don't know what I want.'

Naresh cut in, 'But that day you said that even if the Guru ordered you, you wouldn't marry him.'

A sarcastic observation presented itself to Arti, something about how this topic seemed to have finally drawn Naresh into the conversation, but when she looked at her husband's face, there was an agitation on it that stopped her from airing her comment.

'I know I had, Nareshji,' said Pinki. 'But sometimes I think, maybe that is the right thing. Mummy is getting older and Arjan will also need money for his studies. How much can I do alone?'

'You aren't alone,' said Naresh. 'We are there with you.'

'Yes,' said Arti, 'why do you feel alone?'

Naresh stood up suddenly. His right hand went to his head, his fingers massaging his temple. He sat back down again. His knees hit the edge of the coffee table. The teacups clattered.

'Are you okay, Nareshji?' asked Pinki, springing up.

Arti stood too. 'Do you have a headache?' she asked.

'No,' said Naresh. 'I'm okay. Sit down. Drink your tea. I'm okay.'

The two women sat back down slowly.

'It's your wish,' said Naresh, measuring each word as he spoke it. 'If you think it is the right thing, then you should do it.'

'But Nareshji, you were the one who used to keep telling me to get married. This world is not a good place for a single woman with a child.'

'I'm still saying that.'

'Not since I mentioned Kamaljeet's letter.'

'Really?' said Arti, turning to Naresh. 'You said that you encouraged her, but she was against it.'

'I did encourage her,' said Naresh.

Pinki, who could have contradicted this claim, did not. Her silence convinced Arti that Naresh hadn't, in fact, encouraged her.

'What is wrong if she wants to marry Kamaljeet?' she asked. 'Why are you discouraging her?'

'I didn't discourage her,' said Naresh.

'He didn't, Bhabhi,' said Pinki.

'A woman alone,' continued Arti, ignoring Pinki's interjection, 'a small child, an old mother. What support does she have? Yes, you are there and I am there, maybe some other well-wishers, but finally it is all on her, isn't it? Every house needs a man.'

'For what?' asked Naresh.

'For what? What do you mean for what?' said Arti. 'For everything. To earn. To take care of the children. To make a life for the family. What else?'

'What if the man is useless?' asked Naresh, his tone remaining even in the face of Arti's rising pitch.

'Kamaljeet is not useless,' said Arti. 'He works hard and earns well. I'm sure he doesn't have any bad habits either.'

'I am not talking about Kamaljeet,' Naresh said, standing up again.

'Then who are you talking about, Nareshji?' asked Pinki. She looked towards Arti in puzzlement.

Arti was staring at Naresh with her mouth open, her lips quivering. 'Where are you going?' she asked. There was a tremor in her voice.

Naresh looked at her with still eyes. Then he turned and walked out of the room.

Pinki stood up and walked over to Arti. 'Bhabhi,' she whispered, running her hand over Arti's back. 'Don't worry, Bhabhi. Everything will be all right.'

Naresh pushed his way through the glass doors of the entrance to the shiny building that he had seen several times from the Gurgaon Expressway – never imagining that he would one day enter it – and was immediately cooled by the silent air-conditioning that filled the large atrium on the ground floor. To one side was a concierge's long desk in black marble, directly across from a bank of elevators whose silver-coloured doors shone as if they were polished more than once a day. Embossed in large mauve lettering onto the wall directly in front of him were the words 'Bhan Group'.

The girl at the desk wore the kind of clothes that he had seen flight attendants and staff at five-star hotels wear. She spoke to him in Hindi with an accent that made it clear to him that the people she spoke to in English were better than he was. At first, she found it hard to believe that he – she used the respectful 'aap', but looked him up and down in a way that undermined the word – thought he could meet Mr Khanna, special advisor to Mr Bhan. But when Naresh insisted, she asked him if he had an appointment. He didn't. But, he pleaded, if she called Mr Khanna, he would definitely not refuse to see him. Either not wanting to risk the possibility that Mr Khanna actually wanted to see this balding and somewhat bedraggled man, or taking pity on his appearance, the girl picked up the phone and dialled a number.

'What did you say your name was?' she asked, covering the receiver with her hand.

'Naresh Kumar.'

'From?'

The question hit Naresh harder for its brevity. Everyone always asked this question and it was the answer that made you something or nothing. Was he, under suspension, allowed to tell this girl that he was 'from' the department? He had read the suspension rules several times over the years for one reason or another, but he couldn't remember anything there that would help him either tell this girl that he was from the department, the way he had answered the question all these years, or tell him clearly that his authorisation to use that affiliation to identify himself had also been suspended. Maybe, he thought, he should get a copy of the suspension rules and read them again.

'From?' asked the girl again, but before he could respond, the person at the other end of the line picked up the phone. 'Hello, Aastha,' she said. 'This is Renu. There's some Naresh Kumar from, umm, to meet Mr Khanna.'

When the door shut silently behind him and he turned, Naresh saw that Khanna's office was at least as large as Mr Asthana's and much better appointed: the desk appeared to have ornately carved legs, the room's carpeting was wall to wall, there was a real plant in one corner, and the windows were wide enough to provide a panoramic view of the highway rolling by and thick enough to screen out the sound of the traffic. As the luxuriousness of the room unfolded before him, Naresh felt like he had been tricked. Khanna had always met Naresh in Naresh's office and he had met him like he was an equal – almost a supplicant – like they were both sidekicks to important men, and hence of the same tribe. He had never indicated that he actually sat in an office as lavish as this. The sight of it made Naresh realize that everything he had thought he would say to Khanna was meaningless. He had rehearsed the wrong lines.

Khanna was leaning over a small rectangular object that looked like an elaborate mobile phone, except it didn't have any buttons and had a very large screen. He was poking the screen with a dark pen-like thing. 'Nareshji,' he said without looking up, 'come in.'

'Namaste, Khanna Saheb,' said Naresh, stepping up to the desk, realizing a moment too late that he had never before addressed Khanna as 'Saheb'.

'Bhan Saheb insisted I buy this,' Khanna said, pointing to the phone. 'He said, enough of that old Nokia with a black-and-white display. And enough of doing everything by phoning up people. From now on, check your email on this.'

Naresh nodded and smiled ingratiatingly, not knowing what to say, then realized that Khanna wasn't looking at him and said, 'It's true.'

'Why are you standing, Nareshji?' said Khanna, when he finally looked up. 'Please sit. Can I have them bring something? Tea? Something cold?'

The device that Khanna had been prodding rang now and its owner picked it up. Greeting the person at the other end effusively, Khanna indicated to Naresh with his finger that it would take a minute. But soon the conversation settled into a rhythm and there was no option but to wait. This was familiar, this waiting at a powerful man's desk while he went about his work. Naresh had been on both sides of the desk, he knew what it was about. He knew that Khanna could easily ask the caller to call back later. When Khanna had been on this side of the desk in Naresh's office, Naresh had made him wait too. The memory of those occasions made Naresh smile – it was necessary to make people wait, otherwise they thought less of you. But then the thought came to him that in the last twenty years he had waited at many desks and many people had waited at his desk, but this was the first time he had become a supplicant to a person who had once supplicated to him.

'Don't worry about this inquiry-shinquiry, Nareshji,' said Khanna, when he finally put the phone down.

'I am not worried about that,' said Naresh. He was worried about it, but he didn't want to discuss the inquiry with Khanna.

'Your Asthana Saheb is not one to go down without a fight. And then Bhan Saheb is there to help.'

'I am sure he will. I'm not worried about that.'

'Has the inquiry started?'

'They have sent some notice.'

Khanna waited for him to continue, but Naresh had nothing more to say. 'Did you want to talk about something else?' he asked finally.

'Yes,' said Naresh, then stopped again.

'What is it, Nareshji?'

'It's been six weeks,' Naresh began slowly, his eyes fixed on the desk in front of him, 'and there has been no word about the shop.'

'Shop?' asked Khanna. 'What shop?'

'In Gurgaon. The shop. For Praveen. My son. You had said that within a month you will send the papers and he can apply.'

'Oh,' said Khanna, snorting with laughter. 'That shop. Forget about that shop, Naresh Bhai.'

The words, delivered casually, hit Naresh like a punch to the stomach, no less of a shock because he had seen it coming. He had feared something like this for some time now. The idea that Khanna was going to back out, one way or another, had been niggling at the back of his head. Why had he made a fool of himself by coming here, he thought. It had been so obvious. Now that he and Mr Asthana were suspended, he was useless to Mr Bhan and to Khanna.

'Nareshji? What are you thinking, Nareshji?'

'Nothing,' said Naresh, getting up from the chair.

'I'll tell you what you are thinking,' said Khanna, also standing up. 'Khanna is a snake. Khanna has stabbed me in the back.'

'I'll go, Khanna Saheb,' said Naresh, turning.

'First hear me out at least, Nareshji. That project has been stopped by the Haryana government. Some violation of something they just discovered. The building site has been sealed.'

'Oh,' said Naresh, responding more to Khanna's pausing for breath than to the facts being stated.

'Do you know why?'

'No.'

'The party at the centre is also the party in power in Haryana, Nareshji,' explained Khanna, with the glee of a gambler laying out a winning hand. 'Your minister is also the general secretary overseeing the Haryana unit of the party.'

'Oh. But what violation did they find?'

Khanna regarded Naresh indulgently. 'You know better than me, Nareshji, that these rules and codes serve only two purposes. One is to make all of us feel like our government is regulating things, looking after our concerns, keeping us protected. And the other is to give them a big stick with which to beat us. And they beat all of us with it, from the beggar on the street to someone like Bhan Saheb. The difference is this: who can take the beating and live, and who dies when the blows begin to land.'

The truth of Khanna's words made Naresh nod involuntarily. He took a deep breath and said, 'What should we do now?'

'For now forget about the shop,' said Khanna, smiling at Naresh's 'we'. 'Maybe once this storm passes, the project will restart.'

'But when will the storm pass?'

Something in Naresh's voice made Khanna head turn to him sharply. Naresh saw Khanna's puzzlement turn to something that closely resembled pity.

'Have faith, Nareshji,' said Khanna finally. 'The storm will pass.'

Arti walked up to the bank of ice-cream pushcarts parked at the side of the wide intersection. Behind the white neon-lit ice-cream vendors stood the imposing but mellow stucco of India Gate, illuminated in yellow by the sweeping beams of light. On the neatly planned lawns surrounding India Gate, families sat picnicking in the cool night. Cheap Chinese toys glowed blue and green against the dark shapes of their owners. The sounds of children playing rose and fell.

'One chocobar,' said Arti, then turned to Naresh and asked, 'do you want something?'

Naresh shook his head. Turning from her, he stood with his back to the monument, looking up the long wide road, Raj Path, that led away from it westwards, flat for almost a kilometre before climbing Raisina Hill, passing through the fjord created by the two Secretariat buildings and terminating in Rashtrapati Bhavan – the palace from where the people of India exercised their sovereignty on their country through the ceremonial figure of their President, usually a tottering old man who was there because of his long history of loyalty to the people who actually held power. The two secretariat buildings were not lit, but their domes stood out black against the night. An architect's mistake, made a century ago, meant that Naresh could not actually see Rashtrapati Bhavan from where he stood because the slope up the hill was too steep. But he could feel the presence of that building. Its monumental power came pouring down the road, spilling onto the lawns on either side. His pupils dilating as they focused on the dark shapes at the far end, Naresh felt his eyes tingle as tears rose in them. A thought leaped out of his mind; escaping the clutches of reason, it ran up Raj Path. He would bang his fist against the iron-grilled gate of Rashtrapati Bhavan. He would beg for an audience with the President. I work for your government, he would say, I work at your pleasure. I am your servant, I have served your government for more than two decades and today your government has cast me out like a dirty rag. I am innocent, he would say, falling at the President's feet. I have done nothing wrong. You are the father and mother of all Indians, you know what it means to have children. Everything I did was for my wife and children. Wasn't it my duty to feed them and clothe them?

'What are you thinking?' asked Arti.

Naresh turned with a start towards his wife, who stood with her neck extended forward to prevent the rapidly melting vanilla ice cream from trickling over the chocolate shell and dripping onto her sari. 'Nothing,' he said.

'You were thinking of something,' said Arti, her tongue running up the side of the bar, interrupting the white streams on their way down.

'I was thinking I should contact Bhutani.'

'AIIMS Bhutani?'

'Yes.'

'For Seema? Or for something else?'

'What else can he do for me?' snapped Naresh.

'I thought we had discussed this already. Hadn't we decided that it doesn't make sense to try and interfere? Ashok is getting her treated. So what if this attempt didn't work? It will happen.'

'When will it happen? When it's too late?'

'What do you mean, too late?'

'You know what I mean.'

Arti looked at her husband's profile. He had turned back towards Rashtrapati Bhavan, his eyes fixed on a distant point.

'Let's walk that way,' said Arti.

They strolled up the road, Naresh's heavy steps crunching the red sand that was laid on the sidewalks. 'AIIMS is the best hospital in India,' he said. 'The best doctors in India.'

Arti cleaned up the remaining ice cream. She looked around for a place to discard the wooden stick she was left holding. Not finding one, she threw it onto the lawn, where it took its rightful place in the patchwork of rubbish that accumulated here every evening. 'AIIMS is very far from their house. It can take two hours just to come one way.'

'She can come and stay with us for a few days.'

'With us? Have you gone mad?' Arti stopped mid-step.

'What is mad about her coming to her father's house for a few days?' asked Naresh, walking a few steps ahead, then turning and facing her.

'Do I have to tell you this as well? A girl who has come to her father's house cannot go back to her own till her husband comes and takes her.'

'All these are old-fashioned notions,' said Naresh, although he realized immediately that Arti had caught him out. He hadn't thought of that at all.

'And you are very new-fashioned.'

Naresh gestured with his hand and they started walking again. 'Ashok will take her when it's done. He is not that kind of person,' he said.

'What do we know about what kind of persons they are? It's only in difficult times that you find out what a person is truly like. Aren't we now seeing what kind of people they are?'

'Don't make a mountain out of it. They want a grandchild and they are unhappy because it is taking time. What is unusual about that?'

'Yes,' said Arti, an inapposite amusement entering her voice. 'I am the one making a mountain out of it. Sometimes you are so blind to what you yourself are thinking.'

'I am a father after all. If I don't worry about my child, who will?'

Unexpectedly, this silenced Arti.

'I have decided,' said Naresh, thinking that his assertion had won him the argument, 'I will talk to Bhutani. Seema can come home for a few days while the treatment goes on. The doctors at AIIMS are the best in the world, they will cure her.'

And the credit for curing her will go to you, Arti said to herself. The scheme was half-baked. Maybe the doctors at

AIIMS could do something that the other doctors hadn't done. But was it really likely? And it was not like earlier now. Today there were good doctors in every corner of the city. The fancy new private hospitals that Ashok had taken Seema to were known to have some of the best doctors in Delhi, many of them lured away from government hospitals by much higher salaries and better facilities. It didn't make sense to think that AIIMS was the answer. But, Arti realized, logic wasn't the motive force behind Naresh's thinking.

'Let's go back,' she said, stopping.

'But I …' Naresh raised one hand towards Rashtrapati Bhavan.

'I'm tired,' said Arti.

'Okay,' said Naresh, his hand falling back to his side.

They walked in silence to where Naresh had parked his scooter. He unhitched his helmet by unlocking the luggage compartment and put it on.

'Tell me one thing,' Arti said just as Naresh began to kick-start the scooter. 'This baby-making process, doesn't it involve Ashokji also? How can she conceive if she is here and he is there?'

'He can also come and stay with us,' said Naresh, taking his foot off the pedal. Then, realizing how ridiculous his suggestion was, he said, 'I mean, no, he doesn't have to come. He just has to come when they want his sample. And if the doctor says she has to be with her husband, she can stay here two-three days and go back there.'

'How can she do all this if Ashokji doesn't agree?'

Naresh put his whole weight on the kickstarter. The scooter's engine sputtered into life. 'He will agree. Why won't he agree?'

They were on their way home, speeding through night-time's light traffic, Arti sitting behind Naresh – with both her legs on one side and an arm wrapped around his waist, her sari's pallu wrapped tightly around her hair – when another thought struck her. 'This Bhutani,' she yelled into the side of the helmet, 'how well do you know him?'

Naresh turned his head and said something, but the scooter was at a high speed and his words were lost in the slipstream.

'How do you know,' Arti yelled, even louder this time, 'that he hasn't heard about your suspension?'

The scooter's engine – it had been at full rev – cut off suddenly as if the throttle had been abruptly released. Then the throttle jerked open again and the machine roared forward, its front tyre rising off the road and falling back on it with a thud as it resumed the journey south.

Through the gaps in the tall green hedge that skirted the lawn, Naresh could see the first and last pages of the day's newspaper standing vertical in mid-air in front of a glass-topped wicker table that held a china teapot and a cup and saucer. The fingers of two hands were visible on either side of the paper, holding it up: clean, fair-skinned hands. A gold ring with a large garnet set in it shone on one finger. The stone drew Naresh's eye. He had not seen Mr Asthana wear anything like it in all these years. For a moment, he thought he had come to the wrong house. Then the hands holding the newspaper executed a practised motion, coming together to turn the page, and their owner came into view. It was Mr Asthana.

Naresh walked to the grilled metal gate and cleared his throat. The newspaper did not move. He coughed and cleared his throat again. The newspaper came down.

'Oh Nareshji,' said Mr Asthana. 'I was going to call you. Good you came.'

'Namaste, sir,' said Naresh, folding his hands.

'Why are you standing there? Come in.'

Naresh indicated the gate's fastened latch and smiled apologetically.

'Oh. The gate.' He turned his head towards the open door leading into the house and called, 'Ramkumar, open the gate for Nareshji.'

Ramkumar appeared after a while, wiping his hands on a dirty apron. He greeted Naresh with a nod and unlatched the gate, letting him in.

'How are your daughters, sir?' asked Naresh, sitting down and gratefully accepting the cup of tea Ramkumar offered him.

'Just the other day, the younger one, Ayesha, sent some

photos from their trip to Hawaii. Ramkumar, bring my laptop from the study.'

The laptop's screen was barely visible in the bright light of the sun, but Naresh kept his neck craned and nodded politely. They spent the next fifteen minutes going over the photographs in minute detail, Mr Asthana explaining the topography of the Hawaiian Islands, the technical details of surfing, the culture of beachside holidays in America and other such matters, while Naresh squinted to make out images of deep blue water, shining sands, insubstantially clad, fit-looking people and Mr Asthana's younger daughter and son-in-law posing in dark glasses and caps.

'She's going to have a baby in six months. They say they're going to call him Neil if it is a boy, short for Indraneil. What do you think?'

'It's a very nice name, sir.'

'Mrs Asthana and I are thinking of spending a few weeks with them in Santa Clara,' said Mr Asthana, putting the album down. 'If the government has seen it fit to grant me leave without my asking for it, I should take advantage of it. What do you think, Nareshji?'

'But sir,' said Naresh. 'What about the inquiry?'

'What about the inquiry?' asked Mr Asthana, putting the laptop down and pouring himself some more tea.

'How can you go away when the inquiry is on?'

'Why can't I go away?' asked Mr Asthana. 'Don't give these things so much importance, Nareshji. In any case, the committee has given me one month to file my reply to their notice. And the reply is what, nothing. I deny the charges completely. Such a simple reply that I don't even need you to type it for me. I'll type it myself on my laptop and send it to them once I'm back.'

'And my reply?'

'I'll take care of that. I've got a copy of the notice they sent you. I'll have a reply made to that as well. Ramkumar will bring it to your house so that you can read it and sign it.'

'How did you get …' began Naresh, stopping short when he saw the smile on Mr Asthana's face.

'Don't look so worried, Nareshji,' said Mr Asthana, leaning back in his chair. 'I met Babaji recently. Do you know Babaji? His ashram is near Palwal. He is the one who told me to wear this garnet. Babaji read my charts and assured me that everything will be fine.'

Naresh nodded. He knew who Babaji was. All of Delhi knew that Cabinet ministers and prominent Opposition leaders alike took Babaji's counsel. By going to Babaji, Mr Asthana had clearly taken his case to a very high authority.

I should feel reassured, Naresh thought to himself. But he didn't. 'Babaji saw your chart, sir. Not mine.'

Asthana threw his head back and laughed. 'Nareshji,' he said, smiling broadly. 'Many of the houses of your chart overlap with the houses of mine.'

A feeling of relief finally seeped into Naresh's body. 'There is one other thing, Asthana Saheb. My son, you have met him, Praveen. He is looking for a job. He has a BA and is very good with computers.'

'If you had asked me a few weeks ago, I could have done something. But right now, I think the best thing to do would be to ask Khanna. You know Khanna, Mr Bhan's Khanna.'

'But ...'

'Okay, leave all that now. I have something important to discuss with you.'

The Bhan Group's latest coup had been securing rights for uranium mining in the Northeast. It was a large project, potentially worth several hundred crores. Mr Asthana had been consulted extensively on various aspects of the bid, helping the Bhan Group to beat out several strong competitors, including big mining companies from other countries. With Mr Asthana now free from his job responsibilities for an indefinite period of time, Mr Bhan had requested him to oversee the starting up of the project. 'Now it isn't possible for me to go and live there, Nareshji. You know my health problems and all. Mrs Asthana put her foot down and said no. When I told Mr Bhan this, he said, don't worry, you can work from Delhi, just find a trusted person who can be your eyes and ears over there. So I thought of you.'

'You want me to go there?' asked Naresh. 'Me?'

Mr Asthana leant forward in his chair and looked straight into Naresh's eyes. His face tilted slightly and his brows scrunched together to form an expression that even the most distrustful person would concede was earnest. 'Who can I trust more than you, Nareshji?'

'But, sir, what about my family?'

'What are you worried about?' asked Mr Asthana. 'Your daughter is married and lives in her own house. Mr Bhan will find your son a good job, and your government house is still there for him to stay in if he wants. As for you and your wife, the main site, where the office is located, is in a small town. You can find yourself a nice big house there, maybe one or two servants to maintain it. The Bhan Group will pay the rent and buy your furniture and TV and all those things.'

'I have never been to the Northeast,' said Naresh.

'It's beautiful, Nareshji,' said Mr Asthana. 'Hills and forests and rivers. It will be good for your health also. You have been looking a little pale these last few months. There will not be too much work for you either. You set up the site office to your comfort and go there for a couple of hours every day. A car will be provided. Once a day, you phone me or I will call you and discuss whatever needs to be discussed.'

A black beetle was climbing one of the legs of the wicker table. Naresh watched it take one step at a time, clutching the cane on its way up. He tried to focus on what Mr Asthana was saying, but it sounded as unreal as Hawaii had looked. His own official car, a house with servants, everything paid for. For him, Naresh Kumar, PA to Shri Asthana, IAS. 'Isn't it unsafe over there?' he asked.

'Only in the really remote areas. This isn't one of them. Even then, you will have protection. Besides, Mr Bhan is very smart. He has already talked to the insurgents who operate in the neighbouring state and paid them off. They like money more than they hate outsiders.'

Some part of Naresh, a vigilant but weak part, realized that he was beginning to like the sound of this offer. From this part came a last ditch effort: 'But, sir, isn't it against government rules to take another job while in service?'

Mr Asthana laughed long and hard at this. When he finally quietened down, he said, 'Nareshji, I am fully aware of your deep respect for government rules.' He laughed once again.

Announcing itself with a vibration, Naresh's phone began to ring in his pocket. 'Sorry, sir,' he said, taking it out and pressing the call reject button without looking at the screen.

'So, what do you think, Nareshji?'

'I don't know, Asthana Saheb.' The phone rang again.

'Take it.'

'No, no,' said Naresh, looking at the screen this time. It was Arti. He rejected the call.

'Look, Nareshji, you may be worried about how long this project will last and what will happen when you are reinstated in your job. The fact is that the inquiry will go on for six months at least. In the meantime, see if you like the place. And let Mr Bhan see if he likes your work. If both sides are happy, you can continue on the project after the inquiry ends, no matter what happens. If you are reinstated, go on long leave for a year till the project lasts. If you are not, then resign from the department and continue there. When the project finishes, we will find something else for you.'

In Naresh's pocket his phone rang again. 'Let me consult my wife,' he said, fumbling to reject the call without taking the phone out. 'I'll tell you in a few days.'

'Don't take too long, Nareshji,' said Mr Asthana, picking up the paper from the table. 'Good opportunities come rarely. When they come, they must be grabbed.'

Naresh called Arti as soon as he was out of Mr Asthana's line of sight. 'What was so urgent?' he said when she picked up.

'Did you say something to Praveen today? Did you scold him?'

'I didn't even see him today. Why?'

'He sent me an SMS saying he is going to Manali for a holiday with some friends.'

'Manali?'

'Yes. It's very strange. He has never gone like this before. He always says that it's very difficult to get leave from his job. And what friends has he gone with?'

'Why don't you call him and find out?'

'I have been trying for the last hour. His phone is switched off.'

4

Ashok surveyed the array of dishes laid out on the dining table in front of him – one dal, three vegetables, paneer and chicken curry and dry mutton, raita, papad, cut salad, a pulao garnished with caramelized onions – and said: 'Mummyji, there was no need for all this.'

'What do you mean no need?' said Arti, coming out of the kitchen with a hot paratha on a plate and laying it down in front of her son-in-law. 'You don't come here every day.'

'If I get this kind of lunch, then I might start coming every day,' said Ashok, breaking into a laugh at his own witticism.

'Yes, yes, you must,' said Arti, smiling broadly.

Naresh picked up the dish in front of him and began to serve himself.

'Ask your son-in-law first,' hissed Arti. 'Starts eating himself as if he is the only one at the table.'

'Ashokji,' said Seema, cutting in, 'would you like to start with the vegetables and dal?'

'Mummyji,' said Ashok. 'Why don't you come as well?'

'Just coming,' said Arti. 'Let me make a few more parathas. You start eating. I'll bring you another hot one.'

Ashok had been hesitant when Seema first told him about Naresh's idea to have her treated at AIIMS. 'There is nothing special about AIIMS any more, there are good doctors everywhere nowadays,' he had said. But when he reluctantly put the idea to his mother, Sarla's response was indifference, so there was no reason not to go ahead with it.

'Bhaiyya had called yesterday,' said Seema, once her mother finally sat down. 'But from some other number.'

'He lost his phone,' said Naresh. 'Said it fell out of his hand, through the window of the car and down the hill.'

It had been five days now since Praveen had left. He had sent text messages every other day from Manali, then Solang. Two days after he went away, he had called and explained that he had lost his phone. He could get another phone, he said, but he didn't have a proof of residence with him and nowadays they were very strict about that. 'I'll be back in ten days, anyway,' he said.

'He's thinking of renting a motorcycle and driving to Leh,' said Seema.

'He'll break a leg, that's what will happen,' said Naresh.

'Always wishing for bad things,' said Arti. 'Especially when it comes to your son.'

'Are you sure he's gone to Manali?' asked Ashok.

'Why?' said Seema. 'Where else would he have gone?'

'No,' said Ashok. 'There was this news item ...'

'That same thing again,' said Seema. 'You are just after my brother.'

'What news item?' asked Arti.

'Nothing, Mummy,' said Seema. 'Just some thought that has lodged itself in his head.'

'What thought?' asked Naresh, a tightness beginning to build within his own head.

'Let it be, Babuji,' said Seema.

'What is it Ashokji?' asked Naresh. 'Tell us also.'

Soon after marrying Seema, Ashok, in his attempt to be a solicitous older brother-in-law had taken an interest in Praveen's career. But Praveen, who otherwise had an evident affection for his sister's husband, had deflected these overtures. When Praveen had begun working at the call centre, Ashok, who did not think much of a call centre as a job option, had tried talking him out of it. Although unsuccessful, he had not completely given up, asking Praveen every now and then how his work was going and what the job was like. In the course of these conversations, despite Praveen's tight-lipped behaviour, Ashok had surmised that there was something not quite right in what his brother-in-law was doing. He mentioned this to Seema, but she had either dismissed his suspicions, or, depending on her mood, become protective of her brother and taken her husband to task for picking on him. Eventually, Ashok had given up, deciding that it was best to stay clear of the matter.

But the morning that he and Seema were to go to her parents' house, Ashok had noticed a news story in one of the inner pages of the newspaper about a girl who had gone missing. She had gone to work on a night shift to her call centre and had not returned the next morning. Instead, her mother had received an SMS from her saying that she was staying over at a friend's house. This, the parents later told the police, was not unusual. Some of her friends from college worked at the same call centre and sometimes she went home with them, especially if they planned to go shopping the next day. Often when that happened, she spent the entire day with her friends and went to work directly from there without coming home. Over the next two or three days, her parents got occasional text messages from her – the police had found out that they were sent from a website and were working on tracking the physical location they were sent from – but her phone was switched off whenever they called, which was unusual. She made excuses over SMS, saying her phone charger was not working and, initially, her parents believed this. But when three days had passed, they contacted the police. It was one of many such stories that appeared in the city pages of the newspaper, but there were two details that leapt out at

Ashok. The girl worked in the same call centre as Praveen. And she had disappeared the same night that Praveen had left for Manali.

'What are you talking about, Ashokji?' asked Arti, the fawning smile she normally favoured her son-in-law with still playing on her face.

'He is not talking about anything,' said Seema. 'Nothing at all.'

Naresh and Arti were both looking towards Ashok. He averted his eyes from theirs and shrugged. 'Yes. It's nothing.'

'There is something,' said Naresh.

'No, Babuji,' said Seema, 'it's nothing.'

'Just something I read in the paper today,' said Ashok, his eyes fixed on his plate. 'She is right. It's nothing.'

'You said something about Praveen,' insisted Naresh, a steady throbbing starting up in his head.

'Leave it, Babuji,' said Seema, trying to appear nonchalant and failing.

Naresh pushed his chair back and walked out of the dining area. When he returned, he had the newspaper in his hand. He folded it open to the page that had the call centre story. 'What did you read in the paper today?' he asked Ashok.

Ashok looked up and saw that his father-in-law had turned the paper towards him. The girl's face – a smile, a lock of hair straying onto her forehead, her arm around an older woman, clearly her mother – was inches from Ashok. He turned his head sharply away.

'The girl who disappeared from the call centre,' said Naresh. There was no questioning note in his voice. 'You're talking about the girl who disappeared from the call centre.'

Ashok began to wish that he had kept his mouth shut. But it was too late now. Naresh had already reached the same conclusion that his son-in-law had. He need not have brought this up, Ashok thought. He should have let it go. He wanted to look away from his father-in-law, this man whose life would fall to pieces if his suspicions were true. But he had spoken now, and the only thing he could do for Naresh was to meet his gaze when this horrible knowledge – not verified factually, but its truth confirmed by his intuition – was presented to him.

A texture of sadness enveloped Ashok, layered with memories of all the times he had met Naresh, all the facial expressions and mannerisms that he had seen and half-remembered, all that he had thought, consciously and unconsciously, about this person, all that he had heard about him and everything he had heard him say. If he had tried to name it, he might have called it pity, but it was something that went beyond pity. 'Babuji,' he said. 'I don't think Praveen has anything to do with that girl.'

Naresh got up from the table. 'Where are you going?' asked Arti, her voice rising. 'Will someone tell me what is happening?'

'Wait,' said Naresh.

Walking over to Arti's side of the table, he pushed the paper at her. She snatched it from him and started reading.

Naresh walked back to his own chair, directly opposite his wife's, and sat down.

A very long thirty seconds later, the paper came down. 'Praveen's name is nowhere in this,' said Arti, her voice shaking. 'The police are questioning the driver.'

'Today they are questioning the driver,' said Naresh. 'Tomorrow they will come here looking for Praveen.'

'It might be just a coincidence, Babuji, lots of people work in that call centre,' said Seema. 'We don't know anything yet.'

'You don't know anything,' said Naresh. 'Your mother refuses to accept anything. But I know.'

'What do you know?' asked Arti. 'You don't know anything.'

'I know everything,' shouted Naresh, his face shining with anger. 'I know everything about what your son does at night.'

Ashok pushed his chair back. It screeched against the cement floor, a loud harsh sound. 'I should go now.'

'But Ashokji,' said Arti, 'you haven't finished eating.'

'I've eaten enough,' said Ashok.

'Ashokji, please,' said Arti, tears welling up in her eyes. 'Please finish your lunch.'

Ashok looked at his wife. Seema, through her bewilderment, raised her hand and gestured for him to sit down. He hesitated for a moment, then sat down, carefully and soundlessly pulling his chair back. Breaking off a piece from the cold paratha that lay on his plate, he started to eat.

'You also eat,' said Arti. 'Finish your lunch.'

Her husband and her daughter responded to this injunction automatically, unthinkingly, the way they had been trained to respond over many many meals cooked and served to them by this woman who sat now, tearful and distraught, in the chair that was closest to the kitchen.

Pinki finished her lunch and went to the cupboard where she usually stored her dishes. 'Ufff,' she said – out loud although there was no one else in the room – when she saw the wax seal on the keyhole. It had been three weeks now since the cupboard, and all other cupboards in the office, had been sealed on the minister's order. But force of habit still made her get up and go to the cupboard some days, those days in which her preoccupation was particularly deep. She came back to her table and organized the dishes on it in as neat a manner as she could manage and picked up a magazine. But today the happenings in the film world did not hold her attention the way they normally did and, after flipping a few pages, she put the magazine back down.

Across the room, the towel Naresh draped over his chair was still in place. It needs washing, thought Pinki. It wasn't the first time she had thought of taking it off the chair and either dropping it off at Naresh's house or taking it home herself and washing it, keeping it ready for when Naresh would return. But somehow, every time she had balked at actually removing it from the chair. Nareshji, she thought, when will you return, Nareshji?

Her mind ran back over the years that she had known Naresh. He had always been so warm, such a good friend to Harkirat and to her. How he helped me when Harkirat went! she thought. Where would I have been without him? In this day and age, where brothers are baying for each other's blood, that someone should go so far out of his way to help a poor widow, it was truly the Guru's blessing. The strange thing was that these two men were so different from each other. Harkirat was a large man, fond of food and physical activity, while Naresh ate sparingly and began taking walks in the evenings only after the doctor told him to do so. Harkirat talked loudly and loved a good laugh, particularly enjoying ribald jokes, while Naresh rarely raised his voice and laughed only occasionally. In fact, Pinki could not recall seeing Nareshji laugh wholeheartedly since Harkirat had died. But all the differences in mannerism and personality paled in front of the biggest difference of all: Harkirat abhorred the small and big corruptions that were present in almost every aspect of the department's functioning. He often related stories of misappropriation and favouritism to Pinki, getting increasingly angry as he spoke. Sometimes he would throw the newspaper across the room when a particularly egregious scam was revealed. But, when it came to Naresh, he rarely mentioned the things that he must have known Naresh was involved in. A few times Pinki – who knew through Harkirat's oblique references that Naresh was known to take money – confronted Harkirat, asked him how he could be so irate about corruption on the one hand and on the other hand continue to be friends with a person he knew was corrupt. Harkirat's brow would furrow. He would sigh and recite a sher by Bashir Badr:

There must have been some compulsion
No one is unfaithful without a reason.

When Pinki expressed dissatisfaction with this response, Harkirat would sigh again and say, 'What do you want me to do? Fight with the whole world?' Eventually Pinki stopped asking, filing this puzzle with the other strange things that men did for reasons that they knew best. And when Harkirat died, the conundrum died with him. Naresh's helpfulness, his rock-like presence, had wiped away whatever traces of antipathy Pinki might have carried within her.

But apart from Naresh's seemingly laxer moral standards – which in any case Pinki was not confronted with while Harkirat was alive – there had been another thing that had bothered her about him in the early days. Pinki knew, as women often do, when a man found her attractive. In the early days she had thought Naresh was one of those men. But as time passed and the relationship between their families grew, that feeling had subsided. He had become like a brother to her and if occasionally he said something, or she spotted him looking at her in a particular way, she dismissed it as a figment of her own imagination, partly because it was not expedient to do anything else. Now again, after Naresh's reaction to Kamaljeet's proposal, the suspicion had come back and this time it would not be dismissed.

Perhaps in the world there is something like true altruism, there are people who give and want nothing in return. After Harkirat died, Pinki had often thought of Naresh as someone like that. His love and regard for Harkirat had turned into generosity once Harkirat died, she had thought then. And maybe that had been true at the time, that what he had done for her had been pure. But now she was unable to shake off the notion that, somewhere within him, Naresh desired her. She had tried to rid herself of this idea. Perhaps he was just upset that she would have to leave India if she married Kamaljeet. Maybe he felt a brotherly attachment to her that he was not ready to break. But this thought did not stick.

The phone on Naresh's desk rang, loud and harsh, breaking the eggshell of Pinki's reverie. It was a long number with an international code that she immediately recognized as Canada. Her hand paused in mid-air over the receiver. Why would someone from Canada call Mr Asthana's office? The phone rang once more and, leaving the question hanging in the air, she picked it up.

'Bhabhi?' said the voice at the other end. 'Pinki Bhabhi?'

Pinki's head began to spin at the sound of the voice. She looked back at the display. Of course, that's why the number had looked familiar.

'Kamal?' she said, into the phone. 'Why are you calling me in the office? Why didn't you call me on my mobile?'

There was silence at the other end.

Because I don't pick it up when he calls, Pinki thought. Aloud, she said, 'Kamal? Hello. Hello.'

'I'm here.'

'What time is it there?'

'Very late.'

'What happened, Kamal?' asked Pinki, suddenly concerned. 'Is everything okay?'

'Yes,' said Kamaljeet. 'Have you made your decision, Bhabhi?'

'What decision?' said Pinki involuntarily, although both of them knew what he was talking about.

'I'm coming to Delhi next month. I just booked my tickets.'

'Delhi?'

'Yes, Bhabhi,' said Kamaljeet, his voice more angry than frustrated, 'Delhi.'

'Where will you stay in Delhi?' asked Pinki, realizing immediately that she had asked a stupid question.

'Your house, Bhabhi. Where else will I stay?'

Pinki put the phone down and stood looking at it for a moment. Then she turned to Naresh's chair and took the towel off it. Holding the towel in her hand she walked out of the main door into the corridor outside, then turned and went back into the office, folded the towel and placed it next to her lunch dishes. Then she left the office. She walked down the stairs, through the lobby – ignoring the receptionist's greeting – into the building's driveway and then through the large double gates, dodging a car that was turning in, out onto the street.

The sun was up over the stucco buildings and construction sites of the CGO complex. Puddles of water had formed on the road, remnants of a shower that Pinki realized she had not noticed in her windowless office. Each side of the road was jammed with poorly parked cars. A few metres from the gate, a cluster of people stood at a shack. In front of it, two autorickshaws were parked. Pinki walked up to them and, placing her hand on the cloth roof of the one nearest to her, said, 'Who is here?'

A man dressed in faded blue took a drag of a bidi, then threw it down on the street and stepped up. 'Where do you want to go?'

Pinki's brow creased. She felt tears well up in her eyes. 'I, I …'

'What happened, Behenji?' asked the autorickshaw driver.

'Nothing, nothing,' she said hurriedly. 'Sorry. I don't want to go anywhere.'

She turned away from the autorickshaw. Fumbling in her bag, she brought out her cell phone. She found Naresh's phone number and pressed call. But instead of putting the phone to her ear, she stood looking at its screen. The small monochrome display had NARESH steady at its centre and the word 'Calling' blinking above it. Anger flooded through Pinki; a sudden, unforeseen rush that climbed through her head. She started punching the red button with her thumb. But just before the phone went blank, she heard a faint ring through its speaker. Putting the phone back into her bag, she looked around her, then walked back in through the gate.

The phone rang. The bag vibrated along with it. Pinki let it ring three times, then she picked it up. 'Hello, Nareshji?' she said, in the sunniest voice she could summon. 'How are you?'

'Pinki? You had called, but it got cut.'

'Oh yes. Sorry. I dialled your number by mistake.'

'Oh. Okay.'

'Okay Nareshji.'

'Is everything okay, Pinki?'

'Yes, yes,' said Pinki, annoyed, and – to her further annoyance – gratified at his ability to see through her facade.

'If you don't want to tell me, it's okay. I'll put the phone down.'

'No, Nareshji,' said Pinki, hurriedly. 'Actually, I got a call. From Kamaljeet.'

'What did he say?'

'He's coming here. Next month.'

There was silence at the other end of the phone.

'Nareshji?'

'Yes, yes. I'm here.'

Pinki waited for him to say something, then realized that he was waiting for her to speak. She sighed.

'Do you want to come here?'

'It's only two-thirty. I can't leave the office right now.'

'I'll come.'

'No, Nareshji, let it be. It won't be right for you to come to the office. Not while you are suspended.'

'Look,' said the doctor, making yet another attempt to hand the envelopes containing Seema's medical reports back to Naresh. 'I have told you ten times, the decision is final. Her chances of success are very low. We can't take her case.'

'But Mr Bhutani assured me …' Naresh began, but before he could finish his sentence the doctor had put the reports down on the table and begun walking away.

'Then go and talk to Bhutani. I have patients to see.'

Seema, who had been standing silently watching her father argue with the intransigent doctor, began picking up the reports and organizing them. 'Come, Babuji. Let's go home.'

It had been two weeks since Seema had come home. Two weeks in which they had made eight trips to AIIMS. After the first consultation, the doctor had asked for a series of tests. Seema had reports for each of the tests, some of them had been done twice. But when the doctor saw the reports, he threw them back across the table. 'This is not worth the price of the paper it is printed on,' he said. 'All these private hospitals are out to make money. You will have to repeat all of these.' After some coaxing he accepted a couple of the reports, but a series of investigations still had to be done. Each one of them involved a trip to this massive hospital, with its long crowded corridors and its interminable queues. Naresh had hinted to Bhutani that perhaps a word with the technicians could take them to the front of the line at some of the labs and every time Bhutani had said he would talk to them, but each time Naresh went up to the counter and said that Bhutani had sent him, he was told to wait his turn. Finally, after ten days of day-long visits to AIIMS, all the investigations were done. Another few days and the results were reported, and eventually the day came when Seema and Naresh were to meet the doctor at the IVF centre. But the doctor had been quite clear. This was an expensive procedure being done at the government's cost. They needed to be convinced that there was a reasonable chance of success. Seema had already undergone a full round of IVF and failed. 'How can we knowingly throw government money down the drain? We also have to answer to someone, don't we?'

Fulminating to himself as he pounded the corridors of the hospital, Naresh led Seema to Bhutani's office in the administrative wing.

'But Babuji,' Seema said when they reached the door on which a plaque carrying Bhutani's name hung, 'what is the use of this? The doctor has already said they will not do it. What can Bhutani Uncle do?'

'What can he do?' asked Naresh. 'What do you mean what can he do? Do you know where he sits? He sits in the Establishment section, he handles the personnel matters of the class one staff – all these doctors. He can do anything if he wants. You think these doctors with all these letters after their names are something? Let me tell you, they are nothing. This Bhutani knows the insides of each of their personnel files. He knows where they live and how long they have lived there, which year they got married, when their children were born. He knows which of their degree certificates are real and which are fake, all the small and big frauds they have committed. He can tell you which minor rule they violated in which year. He is fully aware of who is close to whom in the hierarchy, who is in favour with those at the top and who is out of favour. He can advise you on how to get out of someone's bad books and get into their good books. They all have a leash, these doctors. A long leash, but it is a leash, and the end of the leash is in the hands of people like Bhutani. If that doctor has said no to me today, it's because Bhutani has not pulled his leash hard enough. Because if Bhutani had pulled his leash, he would have sat up on his hind legs. Instead of making me stand and wait for him, he would have asked us to sit at the table and ordered cold drinks for us.'

When they entered the room Seema, primed by her father's description, found her expectations belied by Mr Bhutani's appearance. He was a short man with silvery hair neatly combed to one side over a dark-complexioned squarish face. There was something about his manner, if not his looks, that reminded her of her own father more than anyone else.

'Naresh Bhai,' said Bhutani, not standing up when they entered. 'Please come. How are you?'

'Bhutani Saheb,' said Naresh, the seemingly genuine friendliness in his voice surprising Seema. 'It's all your mercy.'

'This must be your daughter,' said Bhutani, getting up from his chair now.

'Say namaste to Uncle,' said Naresh, as if his daughter were nine years old.

'Namaste Uncle,' said Seema, going around to Bhutani's side of the table and making a feeble attempt to touch the feet that were inaccessible behind the metal of his desk.

'Live long,' said Bhutani, touching her head with his hand. 'Have good fortune.'

'Bhutani Saheb,' said Naresh. 'Her fortune, good or bad, is in your hands.'

'What is this Bhutani Saheb, Bhutani Saheb,' said Bhutani. 'Since when have I become a saheb for you, Naresh Bhai?'

Naresh smiled a forced smile. His daughter could see that he was holding back what he wanted to say.

'Your father and I have known each other for almost twenty years,' said Bhutani. 'Suddenly after twenty years he starts calling me saheb.'

'No, no. It just slipped out by mistake.'

'Thanks to Naresh Bhai, my children don't need to worry about their future. Did he tell you?'

'Yes,' said Seema.

'If the ministry had acquired my father's land for that factory,' said Bhutani, 'I would have got nothing. Instead, thanks to Nareshji, our plot was left out of the plan.'

'With the new factory a whole township came up there,' said Naresh. 'Bhutani's brother built shops on that land.'

'On land that was left out of the factory project because your father advised me to claim that it was prime agricultural land,' said Bhutani, laughing. 'It's your father's brilliance, Beta. He is a genius.'

'Now help my child, Bhutani,' said Naresh, once Bhutani's laughter had died down.

'Arre, Naresh Bhai,' said Bhutani, his good cheer undiminished by the plaintive tone of Naresh's voice. 'It is not in my hands. I told them, he is a special friend, do whatever you can for him. But they also have their rules. See, this is a research centre. They want to take on hard cases, but their rules say that they first have to evaluate the chance of success. And if there has been a previous failed attempt, then that chance of success goes down.'

'But why such a strict rule?' Naresh asked.

'See, Beta,' said Bhutani, addressing Seema, 'in our country we have heard the same thing for sixty years:

population problem, population problem. Naresh Bhai will remember, he is my age, that when we were just children, they organized camps to sterilize people. They sterilized anyone who they could prove was male, whether he was seventy or seven, it didn't matter. Remember that, Naresh Bhai? My mother kept me locked in my room for a week, otherwise I could never have had children. I would not have been worthy of marriage.'

Naresh looked at Seema. But if Bhutani's insensitive remark had hurt her, she did not let it be known. Her eyes remained fixed on her lap.

'Anyway,' Bhutani continued, 'in this country, things have changed enough that the government is willing to invest some money in helping people have children. It's a fraction of the money they have spent over these sixty years in trying to prevent people from having children, but even this small amount of money is viewed with suspicion. The government is a big ship, no Nareshji? Turning it around takes time. There are a lot of eyes on this centre, a lot of questions being asked as to why we should be helping increase the population. We are leaving the past behind, it's true, but there are many of us who still remember it. What do you say, Naresh Bhai?'

'It's true. And some of us who forget it when it is convenient.'

Bhutani leant back in his chair. His eyes were fixed on Naresh's face. A light smile, perhaps involuntary, played on his lips. 'Naresh Bhai, what can I do? A rule is a rule.'

'A rule is a rule!' Naresh roared, leaping to his feet. 'You are telling me that a rule is a rule? Why don't you just slap me in the face instead? A rule is a rule, he tells me.'

The smile vanished from Bhutani's face. 'Naresh Bhai,' he said, his voice having lost its earlier bombast. 'There are two other patients I have referred to the IVF centre. It's very important that they get treated.'

Naresh motioned to Seema to stand up. 'It's okay, Bhutani. I understand. I am number three on your list. I understand.'

'Naresh Bhai,' said Bhutani, also standing up. 'Don't take it this way. All of us have to decide carefully when to throw which card. We are all holding just a few cards in our hands.'

'You are still holding cards, Bhutani,' said Naresh. 'My cards have been snatched from my hands.'

What have you decided? Four words, dark grainy letters standing against the yellow-green backlit screen looked up at Naresh. What was he going to tell Mr Asthana? The SMS had come late the previous night. He had not replied to it then. Mr Asthana would assume he was sleeping. But it was six in the morning now. Soon he would have to send some sort of response. But what was he going to say? Refusing Mr Asthana directly was difficult. Naresh needed his help. But could he actually go to the Northeast? Would Arti agree to leave Delhi, with Seema and Praveen in their difficult situations? But then, he thought, what can I do for them anyway? He had tried to help Seema and in return he had been humiliated again, betrayed by Bhutani who had once claimed that without Naresh he was nothing. And now, despite the fact that Seema was not getting any treatment, Ashok was not showing any urgency in picking her up and taking her home. As for Praveen, he didn't even know what exactly that boy had got himself into. Did Arti understand that with his suspension he had lost the power to help his children? Did she know that whatever he had been was because of his position, his proximity to Mr Asthana?

She had to know. After all, he had always told her everything. He had always made sure that whenever he made some money she knew where it came from, which rule had been broken and what the consequences of being caught could be. Sometimes, in the early years, this had worried her and he had to explain to her why he thought he could get away with it, which person or what circumstances protected him. But, he now realized, he had wanted her to know the extent of his misdemeanours so that she shared his guilt. What he really wanted was for her to know that whatever he did, he did for her and for their children and that, consequently, even if the government rules did not say so, they too were implicated in his actions. And while his punishment would be according to government rules, if he were caught, Arti's penance would be to support him when he needed it, to soothe him and salve him when the blow came. Perhaps he should have explained this more clearly, he thought, but he could have explained it only if he had understood it himself. Perhaps if he had known, he could have made sure she understood – and perhaps then he would not feel so alone now, with this suspension order in his hand.

His mind drifted back to the first few days after Seema had been born: the waking up in the middle of the night, the illnesses that had worried them so much, the constant crying. Everyone had said that after the first three months things would become easier. And here he was, years and years later, still worrying about his children. How many risks he had taken to ensure his children's future! How many rules he had broken! When would he be free of this worry? When would they be able to take care of themselves? Perhaps around the time when he was old, when he was no longer able to take care of himself. Perhaps not even then.

He clambered out of bed, put the phone in his pocket and walked to the bathroom. Standing over the pot, waiting for the pressure to build, he thought: why shouldn't I go to the Northeast? He had come to this city because there had been a job here. That job was now gone. What was left here? Let the children take care of themselves. He and Arti could go there and start a new life, live comfortably on a good salary. Even if the project ended and

Mr Asthana didn't find him something else, he had made enough in these last twenty years to live well in a small town. He could sell the land he owned in Chandigarh, or the house he had built in Panipat. Even after that there would be enough, even if the government didn't give him his pension. As he pulled up his pyjamas, he found himself trying to calculate the total value of all that he had acquired over the years. It must be at least ten times the gratuity and provident fund that the government would have to give him when he retired. No, it is more, he thought. Even if he added thirty years of pension after retirement, he still had ten times as much put away. Let them keep their peanuts, he thought. He had done enough for the government anyway, spending all those years sitting – always sitting – behind a desk. And this is how they treat me, he thought: suspension, disgrace, humiliation.

He pulled down hard on the toilet's handle and watched the water gush forth into the pot. He went back into the bedroom and, fumbling in his pocket, brought out his phone and unlocked its display. He was about to type his reply when Arti turned in her sleep. Naresh brought the phone to his chest in a hurry, extinguishing the screen's green glow. He waited a moment in the dark, listening. She will never agree, he thought. The phone grew heavy in his hand. He returned it to his pocket. Climbing into bed, he lay back, locking his hands behind his head.

A phrase came swimming through his head: I tell her everything. And, for a moment, his mind searched unsuccessfully for a memory of the point in time when this proposition – I tell her everything – had established itself as a truth. Equally fruitless was an attempt to conjure up a time preceding this intimacy. There were specific incidents from his life before Arti that his mind could reconstruct, but those incidents felt prehistoric. He had no memory of how that life had felt. He had no living recollection of what it felt like to not be able to tell Arti everything. Frustrated in its attempts to remember a forgotten past, his mind stepped away from his self and contemplated this intimacy as if it were between some other man and his wife. Telling her everything had been the way he had lived all these years. But wasn't that how all married couples lived? The moment this thought came to him, he chided himself at its naivety. You've seen too much of the world to believe that, he said to himself. But, having said that, he had to admit to himself that he would not know how to go about living a life in which he hid things from Arti. Then why haven't I told her about Mr Asthana's offer? Naresh started at the question. It was as if someone else had asked it.

But, thought Naresh, the news of Praveen's disappearance came that day and so I forgot to mention Mr Asthana's offer. The argument worked for that day, perhaps, but not for the days that followed. Each day has many hours, especially for a man sitting at home with nothing to do. There had been times when he had thought about what Mr Asthana had suggested. And he had known that he could make no decision without first discussing it with Arti. Then why hadn't he told her about it? I don't actually want to take the job, Naresh said to himself. But that was a patently ridiculous argument. If he had not wanted to take the job, he would definitely have told her about the offer. He would have mentioned it to her and told her that he wasn't going to accept it. It would have been five minutes of conversation over tea.

Then there was Pinki's situation. Why did this Kamaljeet have to reappear now, he thought. But then, so what if he had? Why did it matter so much to him? Kamaljeet was a good man. Naresh had met him several times before he had left for Canada and he knew that Kamaljeet was a serious-minded man who loved and honoured both Harkirat and Pinki. If Pinki did decide to marry him, he would treat her well. He would raise her son like his own, he would care for her mother like she was his own mother. And even as Naresh formulated these thoughts in his head, the realization clutched at his stomach that he didn't want Pinki to agree to marry Kamaljeet because that would mean she would be gone forever from his own life. He admitted freely, to himself if not to anyone else, that he had found Pinki attractive from the first time he had met her. But she was his friend's wife and he himself was a married man. And that had meant that, although he occasionally found himself looking at her for a little longer than he should, although he sometimes felt guilty about feeling something like desire for her, it did not bother him particularly. He did not intend to do anything that was inappropriate, that he knew, and so this attraction was a minor niggle, something that could be ignored. When Harkirat died, he had helped Pinki wholeheartedly. It may have been partly because men want to be useful to women they find attractive, or it may have been partly out of guilt for having wanted his dead friend's wife, but it was mainly because of his love for Harkirat. He had been sure of that. But now, this proposal from Kamaljeet had revealed that his feelings for Pinki were not benign. They had a life of their own. They were capable of making him do things that he might not be able to forgive himself for.

I wish I could talk to someone about this, he thought. I admit that I have had these impure thoughts, he would say, but I promise they will remain just thoughts, I will never act on them. And whatever penance can be done for having thought all this, I will do. But there was only one person with whom he could have this conversation, and that person was Arti. How could he tell his wife of so many years that he thought he had feelings for another woman? She would either break down and cry and curse him for betraying her or, and this was somehow worse, be understanding and tell him that it was for him to decide what he wanted to do about his feelings for Pinki. Or was there some other reaction that would come, the product of some aspect of Arti's personality that he did not yet know, something about her that lay hidden beneath and had lain there because nothing had ever happened between them to goad it awake?

His eyelids were drooping now with long-deferred sleep. His head nodded forward. I should send some reply to Mr Asthana, he thought.

But Arti will never agree to going. Even in his sleepy state he realized that his mind had traced a large circle and returned to where it had begun. But if she didn't agree, that meant he could not go. Does it really mean I can't go? How could he go without her? How would he live without her? Who would take care of his meals and his clothes and his house?

Pinki, maybe Pinki.

His neck jerked back at the thought, like someone had popped a flash in his face. Running a hand over his forehead, he tried to calm down, but the blood kept rushing up into his head. He snaked his hand under Arti's covers and placed it on her shoulder. The warmth from her body soothed him and he decided against shaking her awake.

It might have been a minute that he sat touching his wife, or it might have been ten. He brought his hand back out. I'll tell her today, he thought. And if she says no, I'll say no to Mr Asthana. I'll tell him that my wife is against it. He will understand.

Bringing his phone out of his pocket, he typed out a reply. Dear Asthana Saheb, I got your SMS. I will come and talk to you about it at your residence personally at a time of your convenience.

There were two men sitting on the sofa, cups of tea in front of them on the table, when Naresh returned from his evening's walk. Arti and Seema were sitting to one side. It could have been just another social visit by two acquaintances, except for the worried look on his wife's and daughter's faces, and the fact that the two visitors were dressed in the khaki uniforms of Delhi Police, the difference in their status marked by their headgear: the constable's was round, whereas the other person, presumably some kind of officer, wore a peaked cap.

'Babuji,' said Seema, getting up as her father entered, 'these people are from the police.'

'I can see that,' said Naresh.

'My husband is here,' Arti said, addressing the man with the peaked cap. 'Ask him whatever you want to ask.'

'Naresh Kumarji?' the officer asked, standing up as he spoke. 'I'm Sub-Inspector Passi. Namaskar.'

The sub-inspector's politeness took Naresh completely by surprise. He folded his hands in reply, then nodded at the constable who had also come to his feet now, somewhat reluctantly.

'I have some questions for you, Nareshji,' said Passi, sitting back down and picking up his cup of tea.

'Yes, yes,' said Naresh, undecided on whether to continue standing where he stood or to sit down. 'What kind of questions?'

Passi looked over at the women, then looked at the constable and smiled. 'Ummm,' he said, 'it is, you know, hmmm, not something to discuss in front of the ladies.'

Arti stood up. 'Should I bring some tea for you?' she asked her husband.

'No,' said Naresh, walking across the room and sitting down in the chair his wife had just vacated. 'I'll have mine later.'

The three men watched the two women leave the room. When they had disappeared from view, Naresh turned to Passi. 'Now tell me, Inspector Saheb, what questions do you have for me?'

'Your son's name is Praveen Kumar?'

'Yes.'

'Does he work for Infinix Solutions?'

'Yes.'

'Is he at home right now?'

'No.'

'Where is he?'

Naresh didn't answer the question. He looked at the sub-inspector's face, then at the constable. They weren't asking these questions because they didn't know the answers, he realized. They already knew what he knew. 'I don't know. He said he was going to Manali with some friends.'

Passi put his tea down and leant back into the sofa. He stretched. His right hand brushed the wooden back of the sofa. Turning his head he looked at, and appraised, the piece of furniture he was sitting on.

'You know why we are here.' It was half a statement and half a question.

'That girl. The murder.'

'Good. You know.'

'What has that got to do with Praveen?'

Passi turned towards the constable and laughed. The constable's face broke into a wide smile as well. 'Arre, Naresh Kumarji,' said Passi. 'That is what we have come to ask you. What does Praveen have to do with this?'

'Nothing. Praveen has nothing to do with this.'

'Ombir,' said Passi, addressing his companion, his eyes still on Naresh's face. 'Praveen's father says that Praveen has nothing to do with this. Then who killed the girl?'

'The TV channels say that the driver killed the girl, Saheb,' Ombir replied, a faint smile crossing his lips.

'That's true. We have arrested the driver. We have questioned him.'

'Yes, Saheb.'

'Ombir, you were there when we questioned him, weren't you?'

'Yes, Saheb.'

'Naresh Kumarji,' said Passi. 'This Ombir is very good at questioning criminals. I have seen the most hardened ones fall at his feet and tell him everything. Do you know why?'

Naresh looked at Ombir's face. It bore the expression of a man being praised by his superior.

'He is very persuasive,' said Passi. 'That's why.'

'Arre, Saheb,' protested Ombir. He appeared to be blushing.

'Ombir tried to persuade him to confess his crime,' said Passi, ignoring Ombir's interjection. 'I tried too. After a few hours of persuasion, it was Ombir and myself who got persuaded.'

'Persuaded of what?' asked Naresh.

'He is telling the truth,' said Passi. 'He didn't kill the girl.'

The two policemen were looking at Naresh expectantly, as if it was his turn to speak.

'Do you understand what I am saying, Naresh Kumarji?' asked Passi.

'Yes.'

'Good. So then I thought, let me look into this a little more closely. I went through the mobile phone call records. It appears that this girl and your son used to talk regularly, very regularly. So I thought I'll go to this office and talk to Praveen. But when I got there, they told me he is on leave. And do you know when he went on leave?'

'The day after the girl died.'

'Brother Ombir. I think Naresh Kumarji knows what I am trying to say.'

'Yes, Saheb.'

In the days since Praveen's disappearance, in the time since Ashok had brought up the girl's murder over lunch, Naresh had suspected that Praveen had something to do with the murder. But with that suspicion there had been a sliver of doubt, a doubt rooted in hope, in the kind of battered optimism that lives even in the most wretched of people, that refuses to die even when it is beaten repeatedly like a suspected criminal in a Delhi Police lockup. That optimism now died.

Naresh's head fell to his chest. He massaged his temples with his palms, then looked up again. 'My son is a good boy. He has nothing to do with this.'

'Saheb,' said Ombir, speaking without being prompted for the first time, 'I think you should tell him what a good boy his son is.'

'Naresh Kumarji, I didn't want to tell you this. But I think it is important for you to know the whole truth so that you and I understand each other a little better.' Passi's face had taken on a pained expression, like that of a schoolteacher reprimanding a student for not having done his homework. 'The truth is that your son was providing girls to people in exchange for money.'

'Providing girls?'

'Yes, Naresh Kumarji. Providing girls. There are other words I can use for him, but you are a respectable person and this is your house, so don't push me to use those words.'

'What nonsense!' Naresh said, trying to inject genuine indignation into his voice. 'How can you come into my house and say such things about my son?'

Passi's eyes were fixed on Naresh's face. 'Ombir,' he said, slowly, 'I think Naresh Kumarji is pretending to be outraged. I think he already knew that his son is a pimp.'

Naresh's head spun. He looked away from Passi's searching gaze. 'What has that got to do with this murder?' he asked in a quietened voice.

'The girl who died that night. There was a reason why she was talking to your son so often. She was not his girlfriend. You can say she was his employee.'

Naresh nodded.

'You see why we are here.'

'Yes. But even if what you are saying is true, it still doesn't mean that Praveen killed the girl.'

'Arre Naresh Kumarji,' said Passi, getting up and stretching, 'the investigation is just beginning. There are many things we can investigate once we begin. And once we get a warrant and arrest him, we can maybe persuade him to tell us the truth.'

'You don't have a warrant for his arrest?'

'No, Naresh Kumarji,' said Passi, walking to the window and looking out at the gathering dusk. 'Ombir and I haven't come here to arrest him. We have come to talk to you.'

Ombir smiled at the mention of his name. He stood up from the sofa, belatedly remembering that it was inappropriate for him to be seated while Sub-inspector Passi was standing. Naresh stood up too.

'Look at it this way, Naresh Kumarji,' said Passi, turning back from the window and bending down to pick up his cup. 'The driver has been arrested. He has no alibi for the hours after the disappearance. The media is furious with the call centre at the fact that a woman was the last person to be dropped off. Our Commissioner has said that he will personally ensure that the driver is convicted.' He took a sip of the tea. 'This has gone cold.'

'I'll …' Naresh began, but Passi waved his hand, no. 'It's okay,' he said. 'We have to leave soon anyway. So, what was I saying? Yes, I was saying that Ombir and I are the only ones who feel that there is more to this case than the driver. Just the two of us.'

Naresh felt his skin tingle as the import of what Passi was saying came to him. 'Just the two of you?'

'Now we, this Ombir and I, spent a little time finding out about you, Naresh Kumarji. They say that you have a few houses and some pieces of land in some good places.'

'No, no.'

'Come on, Naresh Kumarji,' said Passi, a broad smile on his face. 'You and I are both servants of the people.'

'I am also a servant of the people, Saheb,' Ombir chimed in.

'If in the course of this public service you have gathered a few things,' Passi continued, ignoring Ombir, 'what is wrong with that?'

'Nothing,' said Naresh.

'Nothing!' exclaimed Passi. 'And after all, what is it for? For your family. For your wife and daughter and, of course, for your son.'

Naresh returned to his chair and sat down. It made sense, he thought, to just settle with these blackmailers. He knew that it might not end this line of investigation –

someone else might independently bring it up – but Passi was the investigating officer and, finally, the case was made on the basis of the investigating officer's report. Even if one way or the other, Praveen did get arrested, having Passi on his side would be a big advantage. But from somewhere within there rose some kind of resistance, a voice of anger that told him to fight these bastards if he could.

'But if the Commissioner has already said the driver is the killer,' he said, weighing his words carefully, 'how can you go against him?'

Passi's eyes narrowed. 'We have hundreds of news channels in Delhi,' he said. 'Every day, someone or the other from one of them approaches me. If I give them a few pointers, the story will break in two days. Commissioner Saheb's word is sacred to me, but he will have to retract his statement.'

'My boss is a senior IAS officer,' said Naresh, playing his last card, his voice quivering with the fear that this last card would also be trumped. 'Shri R.K. Asthana.'

'A suspended senior IAS officer.'

Passi gave Naresh his mobile number before leaving. 'Think about it,' he said. 'Let me know.'

Naresh nodded his assent, then, once they had left, turned and went into the bedroom, waving off Seema and Arti's questions. Shutting the door behind him, he took his phone out and dialled Mr Asthana's number. 'Asthana Saheb,' he said, when he heard the voice at the other end, 'I want to go to the Northeast.'

5

'I CAN'T REMEMBER THE LAST TIME YOU TOOK ME TO SEE A movie,' Arti said, possibly for the sixth time, putting her styrofoam plate, loaded with fried rice and chicken Manchurian, down on the only free table in the entire food court.

'Hmmm,' said Naresh, taking the seat across from her.

'Look,' said Arti, lowering her voice and leaning forward, 'that girl is still wearing her chuda.'

Naresh turned to see a woman – fine-featured, pretty rather than beautiful – her elbows resting on the table, a long sequence of red and white bangles studded with shiny stones covering her forearm. She looked no more than twenty. She was gazing into the eyes of a young man wearing a leather jacket and a self-congratulatory expression, who was holding her hands in his.

'Remember when we were in the first year of our marriage?' asked Arti. 'You used to take me to see movies every other week.'

'I still take you out,' said Naresh.

'I can't remember the last time you took me to see a movie,' said Arti. But the sparkle in her eyes undermined the combativeness in her voice.

Naresh realized that her mood was lighter at that moment than it had been or would be. He took a deep breath and said, 'There's something I have to tell you.'

Confidence in a negotiation – Naresh had learnt over years of cutting small and big deals, licit and illicit – came either from conviction or from a belief in the other person's gullibility. With neither at hand, Naresh began to talk of Mr Asthana's offer of a job in the Northeast with the trepidation of a person walking off a beach into the water knowing that he can't swim. He found himself measuring his intonations, telling himself to lean forward or gesture with his hands for emphasis, reminding himself to focus on certain aspects of the proposition – the rent-free accommodation he had been promised, the beauty of hilly regions.

Some way through her husband's narration, Arti put her plastic fork down. She sat back in her chair. As he talked, her head kept turning to the left, not so much to look at the girl with the chuda as to look away from where

Naresh sat. Eventually, her eyes brightened again, but this time with the moistness of suppressed tears.

'So what do you think?' Naresh asked finally.

'Who will take care of you when you are there?'

The memory of the answer he had given himself the last time this question had come up – Pinki – came swirling back to Naresh. 'No, no,' he said, struggling to keep his voice even. 'You will come with me. We will go there together. How can I even think of going without you?'

'Impossible!' exclaimed Arti.

The couple at the next table glanced over. Their hands separated. The girl giggled nervously. Naresh motioned to Arti to keep her voice down.

'I can't leave Delhi,' Arti stage-whispered. 'What about Seema? And who will take care of Praveen once he returns?'

Naresh noticed through the corner of his eye that the people at the next table were still looking in their direction. He turned and deliberately made eye contact with the man, he wasn't much more than a boy, who hurriedly looked away.

'Tell me,' said Arti. 'Who will take care of the children?'

A muffled voice came over the public address system announcing something that, although inaudible to Naresh, seemed to galvanize a large number of people, mainly women, who rose from their tables and began shepherding little boys and girls of various sizes to one end of the cavernous hall, where a man with a mike stood next to an arrangement of cables suspended from the roof. As Naresh watched, a boy was secured into a harness and raised up to a deafening outcry of applause and hooting.

'What haven't I done for these children,' Naresh said, raising his voice to be heard over the noise. 'What haven't I given them?'

Arti, who had also been watching the orchestrated fun, turned back to her husband. 'What do you mean?'

'Do you remember how much we spent on Seema's wedding? All the things we gave Ashokji and his family?'

'Everyone does that. It was our duty as parents.'

'She has her own family now. They also have some duty towards her.'

'Yes,' said Arti, her jaw set. 'They have been doing that duty very well. But forget about that if you want and tell me: what about my son? Day and night I worry about him. Where is he? What kind of bed is he sleeping in at night? What is he eating? Do you care? I keep saying, do something about it. Bring him back home. But you do nothing. Tell me, what have you done for my son?'

'He has gone on his own. No one has kidnapped him.'

'And even if he comes back,' Arti continued, tacitly acknowledging the validity of Naresh's response by changing tack. 'What will he do here? Go back to that call centre? What kind of life is your son leading? At his age we should be looking for a girl for him. What will I tell her parents? Give me your daughter for a boy who stays out all night? Who will knowingly throw their daughter down a well?'

'Mr Asthana has promised that he will get him a job in Mr Bhan's office. No more staying out all night. A proper job.'

'It's all very well to talk about a job. But he should be able to take the job. What about the police? What about the murder?'

'What about it? That Passi asked for some money. I'll give him what he wants. He'll keep his mouth shut. Whatever it is that Praveen did or didn't do, as long as Passi keeps his mouth shut, it doesn't matter.'

Arti was still trying to reply to this when Naresh continued: 'And don't forget, I am suspended. I need Mr Asthana's help, I need Mr Bhan's help. If they have asked me to do something and I don't do it, then why will they help me?'

'Mr Asthana will help you anyway,' mumbled Arti.

'What did you say?'

'You know all his secrets,' said Arti, louder this time. 'He has to help you.'

Naresh balked at this argument. She knows how it works, he thought, she is intelligent enough to realize how these things work and, unexpectedly, he felt proud of her. But another part of him intervened, saying, Of course she knows how it works, I have explained these things to her carefully over the years. That raw girl I married wouldn't have been capable of this kind of analysis.

'Don't forget, we also need the money. Who knows how much Passi will ask for? And what if there are others?

I may also have to spend some money over the suspension thing.'

Arti rose now and began walking towards the escalator. The girl with the chuda, who had long since lost interest in what had been happening at their table, turned as Arti passed by. She raised her hand as if she wanted to say something, then looked back at Naresh with reproach in her eyes. Naresh avoided her gaze, got up and walked with a hurried step in the direction his wife had gone.

They walked past the glass-fronted shops with their elegant displays – unbelievably thin and tall mannequins draped in expensive fabric, embroidered bedspreads and overfilled pillows, leather handbags one to a shelf. Who buys these things? Naresh thought as he rushed past. The question brought him to its answer. These people he jostled by – young girls in tight jeans and elaborate careless hairstyles, teenage boys in overly loose-fitting clothes, older women in elegant or shiny sarees, their husbands dressed down but managing to convey their affluence through a branded belt or a pair of spectacles – these were the people who bought these things. They were people like him, he thought, but only to the extent that they too were human beings who were born, fell ill and died.

He caught up with Arti in the elevator going down to the basement. 'What happened? What did I say that made you leave your food half-eaten and walk away?'

'I think you want to run away.'

Naresh said nothing. He kept looking at her profile, silently willing her to turn her face towards him. 'It's not that,' he said after a while.

'Then what is it?' she asked, turning her face to him now, her eyes ablaze with anger. 'Tell me! What is it?'

'We need to do this.'

The elevator opened and a clutch of people tried to enter even before Arti and Naresh could get out. Irritated, Naresh deliberately jostled the first man into the lift. 'Watch where you're going,' said the man, turning and putting his hand on Naresh's shoulder.

'Sorry Bhaisaheb,' mumbled Naresh.

'Your daughter is in trouble,' said Arti, once they had reached their parking spot. 'your son has the police after him. And you want to run away to some corner of the world.'

'It's all for them,' said Naresh weakly, unhooking his helmet. 'As it is, my pay has been cut in half. Now the police want money to let Praveen off. Where will all this money come from?'

'We have enough money,' snapped Arti.

'We have enough money?' Naresh was incredulous. 'What do you mean we have enough money? Who knows how much the police will extract? And after these two policemen, there will be others. And ...'

'And what?'

Two people who have been married long enough usually know how to make each other cry. And so, because he knew that what he wanted to say next was a potentially crushing blow, Naresh hesitated.

'Why don't you say … and what?' said Arti.

'What about Seema?'

'What about her?'

'Suppose Ashok leaves her …'

Arti's eyes widened in disbelief. Then tears began to roll down her face. 'Don't say such a thing. Don't even think such a thing.'

Naresh was seized with remorse. He looked around. In the distance, two parking lot attendants were chatting with each other. A car was rolling away from them towards the exit. He moved forward and gingerly embraced his wife. 'At least let me show Mr Asthana that I want to help him,' he said tenderly. Seeing her cry made his heart ache, and the ache in his heart made him lie. 'I'll just go there once and see the place. When I come back, if you still feel you don't want to go, I'll say no to him.'

The doorbell rang loudly, but inside Pinki's sleep-filled head it sounded distant and muffled. It rang again and she opened her eyes with a start. The alarm clock by her bed showed 3 a.m. She got up from the sofa and went to the door. 'Who is it?' she asked, her hand pausing on the latch, although she knew who it was.

'It's me, Bhabhi,' said a voice; a familiar voice that sounded like it had travelled not through a wooden door, but across several years.

She unlatched the door and drew it open. In the darkness of the stairwell outside stood a tall man, thinner than she remembered him, his beard thick as it used to be, but showing patches of white. His eyes, when she found the courage to look into them, were filled with the tiredness of something more than a long journey.

'Bhabhi,' said Kamaljeet. 'It's me.'

He made as if to touch her feet, the way he used to earlier, but she flinched, so he decided not to go through with it. She stepped aside and motioned him to come in. 'How are you, Kamal?'

'I'm okay, Bhabhi,' he said, picking up his oversized suitcase and stepping through the door.

Pinki made tea while Kamaljeet took a bath. She brought it into the living room on a tray. He stood up as she came in. Looking up from the tray, Pinki saw him dressed in a fresh white kurta-pyjama and her feet stopped moving under her. Her dimming memory of her husband's living face, the family resemblance between the cousins, the extra years that Kamaljeet had added since she last saw him – whatever it was, he looked so much like Harkirat had before he died, a thinner body but the same face, that Pinki's sleepy mind lost its grasp of the present. The sound of cup rattling against saucer brought her back. Her hands were shaking. She took a firmer grip on the tray and walked into the room.

They sat in silence as Kamaljeet drank his tea. Pinki thought of asking him how his journey had been, but a wave of drowsiness hit her and when it passed she couldn't remember if she had already asked him the question or not. He asked about Pinki's mother and Arjan. She told him they were sleeping, forgetting to add that they had both been very excited that he was coming. Once these niceties had been navigated in a haphazard manner, silence fell, except for the slurping sounds of Kamaljeet drinking hot tea.

'You are sleepy, Bhabhi,' he said when he finally put his empty cup down. 'Go to sleep.'

'You should also sleep,' Pinki said, beginning to rise from her chair.

'I slept a lot on the plane. It's the middle of the afternoon in Vancouver.'

Pinki sat back down. A sudden wakefulness hit her unexpectedly and, in that wakefulness, the improbability of the situation – Kamaljeet sitting in her house, right there, across from her – came crashing down on her. Had he really come here from Vancouver, a place that she knew only from a map and from the photos he used to send, a place that was thousands of kilometres away? And what did that mean: thousands of kilometres away? Why had it appeared so far away just hours ago and why did it now appear so insignificant?

'I know what you are thinking, Bhabhi. How did this thought come into his mind? Why suddenly after so many years this strange idea? The truth is, I don't know myself how or why this happened. But, and really, I swear on the Guru's name, I tried to dissuade myself for a very long time before I said anything to you. I really tried. It was only after all my attempts had failed that I had to accept that this was the correct thing to do.'

He paused for a breath and looked at Pinki, but her eyes were fixed on the empty cup of tea sitting on the tray.

'The first time I had this thought, I couldn't believe it had come into my mind. For two nights after that I couldn't sleep. I didn't eat a thing. My stomach would keep knotting up. I had diarrhoea every two hours. It was like my whole body had gone mad. Finally I went to the gurdwara. When I reached there it was shut. I looked at the watch and realized it was the middle of the night. I went back and sat in my car till the morning came and they opened the doors. That whole day I prayed and by evening some calm came to me. I went home and ate, and I slept. For the next many weeks I didn't even think about it. Whenever I felt the thought was coming to me, I would start singing Gurbani, and I would keep singing it till I felt the danger had passed. You remember there was a time two years ago when I didn't phone you up for two months, then later told you that I had been ill and was trying to save money because I wasn't able to work much. That was the time. I couldn't call you up. If I had heard your voice at that time, I don't know what would have happened to me.'

Pinki's head jerked forward. She rubbed her eyes.

'Bhabhi, you are falling asleep,' Kamaljeet said, getting up. 'Go to sleep.'

'No, no. Say what you have to say. I am listening.'

Kamaljeet hesitated, then sat down. 'I know what you will say. Why don't you find a nice girl and settle down with her? And actually, in the early years, there were several opportunities. People I met there introduced me to their granddaughters or nieces, some showed me photos of girls from their villages. They liked me there. They saw I was hardworking, I went to the gurdwara every day, I never drank or had any of the other bad habits that some of the unmarried boys who drove taxis had. I must have appeared like the perfect son-in-law to them. But no girl ever measured up to what I had in mind. And, do you know the funny thing, I didn't even know in all those years that what I had in mind was you. I just kept saying no for one reason or the other. In fact, I got angry when people showed me photos, because I didn't want to hurt someone by saying no to her. After a while, they understood that there was something holding me back. Other people understood that before I understood it. Isn't that funny?'

'Hmmm,' said Pinki, trying, with little luck, to focus on what he was saying. The drone of his voice was lulling her into ever deeper sleep.

'I don't know if you have met many people who visit from Canada, Bhabhi. When they are here, they talk about how happy they are. They fill big suitcases with presents and bring them over. I have seen how it is on the other side: the trips to the malls just before taking the flight, the long lists of relatives and friends who have to be given something. And it began to feel like those gifts were to distract them from the simple evident fact that we are all unhappy there. We are all lonely there. And I am not just talking about the boys who are there by themselves away from their families, those who are unmarried or whose wives haven't got a visa yet. I am talking about everyone. Everyone there is lonely, Bhabhi. And I am not talking only about the Punjabis or the Indians or the Chinese or the other immigrants. I am talking about everyone. The whole country is full of people sitting alone in their houses, or clutching on to two or three family members, one or two friends. Sometimes I feel like they go shopping out of desperation, as if they will find something in some shop that will take away their loneliness. But it doesn't go away, Bhabhi. Loneliness is like the cold, Bhabhi, it enters your bones and then no matter how hard you rub, it doesn't leave.'

Pinki's head had fallen to her chest. Her breath was even, a light regular snore. Kamaljeet got up and walked over to her. He touched her on the shoulder.

'Bhabhi. Come, Bhabhi. You need to sleep.' She didn't stir. He put his arm around her shoulder and tried to get her to stand up.

'What are you doing?' Pinki slurred. 'Take your hands off me.'

'Sorry, Bhabhi,' said Kamaljeet, almost jumping back.

Pinki staggered to her feet. 'It's very late,' she said, looking away from him. 'Arjan will wake up in a few hours. His school bus comes early.'

'Yes, Bhabhi. I'm sorry. I shouldn't have kept you up.'

'No, no,' said Pinki walking slowly towards her room. 'Sleep now. If you need anything, just knock on my door.'

Arti picked up the kadhai from the pile of dishes that lay in the sink. Metal plates slid, spoons fell out of bowls and scummy water splashed everywhere at this tectonic shift.

'What are you doing, Mummy?' The voice came from behind her.

'She's not coming today,' said Arti, turning to see Seema standing at the kitchen entrance. 'Her son is ill.' The pronoun was unambiguous: she was talking about the dishwashing lady. 'I can't leave the dishes in the sink overnight.'

'Can I help you?'

Even when she was barely ten years old Seema had wanted to join in, even take over, various household chores. 'It's good,' Arti would tell people, 'what she's learning will help her when she goes to her own house.'

By the time she turned sixteen, Seema had made it her sole responsibility to make chapattis in the evening.

Occasionally she would cook the main vegetable for the night's meal, carrying it to the table herself and setting it down in front of her father who would always praise it, even when she had added too much salt or burnt the tempering. But since she had come back this time, she had not come into the kitchen even once, spending her time in her room – the one she had shared with Praveen before she got married, the one in which she now slept alone amongst Praveen's things – flipping through old issues of women's magazines, or just lying in bed with her eyes shut.

'Of course, Beta. But you don't have to. I can do it myself.'

Seema took the kadhai from her mother. 'This kadhai is in bad shape, Mummy,' she said. 'Its wooden grips are in pieces and its bottom is completely black.'

'I keep telling her to scrub it properly, but she does what she wants.'

'Why don't you throw it away? Buy a new one.'

'I could buy a new one,' said Arti, blushing, 'but I can't throw this one away.'

'Why?'

'This was the first thing your father bought after I came to his house,' said Arti, smiling. 'It's older than you are.'

Seema smiled too, and Arti saw that the smile had somehow deepened the sadness in her eyes.

'Mummy,' said Seema, picking up the metal scrubber, dipping it in soap powder and beginning to scrub the bottom of the now upturned kadhai. 'He had called.'

'Ashokji had called,' said Arti, trying and failing to mute her excitement. 'What was he saying?'

'No, nothing. He had called just like that.'

'Oh,' said Arti, realizing immediately that if her son-in-law had called for no reason, her daughter would not have been telling her about it.

'He was asking about Bhaiyya,' said Seema, her eyes still on the kadhai. 'I told him he hadn't returned yet.'

Arti sighed.

'He said he would make a few enquiries.'

'He is a good man,' said Arti, hesitantly. Then, with more conviction, she continued, 'And he is a powerful officer, Ashokji. I am sure he will be able to help us.'

'I haven't been much help to you. Just lying around the house all day.'

'Beta,' said Arti, her hand moving to take the scrubber from her daughter. 'Your being here is the greatest help your mother can ask for.'

'Hmmm,' said Seema, turning the kadhai in her hand and continuing to scrub it.

'Is there anything else?' asked Arti, her hand returning to her side.

'He is coming day after tomorrow.'

'Ashokji is coming! When? Will he have dinner?'

'Day after tomorrow. Yes, he will have dinner. Actually ...'

'I knew it,' Arti cut in. 'I knew he wouldn't just leave you here. Have you begun packing your clothes? I have a sari for Sarlaji, you must remember to take it with you.'

Seema bowed her head. Her hand moved more vigorously over the kadhai.

'What happened? This is good news. Isn't it?'

'He is not coming to take me home,' said Seema, her hand coming to a halt, the metal scrubber resting on the kadhai.

'Why? Why isn't he taking you home?'

'You should ask him that question,' snapped Seema.

Arti put her hand on her daughter's shoulder. 'Seema,' she said. 'My Bitiya. If he is not coming to take you home, then why is he coming? Is there something he wants to tell us?'

Seema put the metal scrubber back on its nail and turned to face her mother. 'No, Mummy,' she said, removing her mother's hand from her shoulder, cupping it in her two hands, then letting it go. 'It's something else.'

'What is it?' asked Arti, tilting her head as she tried to look into her daughter's averted eyes.

'He is going to stay the night,' said Seema, turning again to protect her eyes from her mother's gaze.

'Stay the night? Here?' Arti asked, incredulous. Ashok had never stayed the night in his wife's parents' home.

'Yes.'

'Why?'

'You don't want him to stay?'

'Beta,' said Arti, 'you know that my son-in-law is the most important guest this house can ever welcome. So don't ever think I don't want him to stay if he wants to.'

'I know,' said Seema, and started to walk out of the kitchen.

'Seema,' Arti said, in a tone that her daughter must have first heard so long ago that she had no memory of having first heard it, a tone that did not allow her to walk away. 'Tell me why Ashokji is coming to stay the night here.'

Seema turned. 'He wants to sleep here.'

'Why can't he sleep in his own house?'

'He wants to sleep with me.'

'With you?' Arti asked. Then her brow cleared and a smile came to her face. 'Oh! So this is what is going on. My own daughter wants to do naughty things right here in her own house, under her parents' noses.'

She stepped forward and gestured with both her hands around Seema's face, taking the evil eye off her. Then she put her hand on her daughter's head and stroked her hair. Running her palm down her cheek, she brought her fingers together and kissed them. 'Of course, Bitiya. Whatever his mother is like, I know our son-in-law still loves my beautiful daughter.'

'No, Mummy,' said Seema, smiling despite herself. 'It isn't that.'

'It isn't?'

'No. He is coming and it is for what you think it is. But the reason isn't what you think it is.'

'Now I am confused. Is he coming for … or not?'

'He is. But it's because the doctor said so, not because of me.'

'The doctor said so?'

'Yes. We count the days. There are three days in the cycle which are supposed to be the best days to conceive. Those three days we make it a point to try each night.'

'Oh.'

'Nowadays we only try on those three nights. And even on those three nights, it has become like catching a train. All he cares about is where we want to go, not how we get there.'

'Is he rough with you?' asked Arti, a current of protective anger flowing under her voice.

'No, Mummy,' said Seema, her eyes crinkling with love for her mother as she spoke. 'Your son-in-law is not like that. It's just that earlier it was different.'

'It was different earlier?'

'Yes, Mummy,' said Seema, now smiling with her eyes as she remembered a time not so long ago, whose passing she had noted only once it had passed completely. 'When I first went to his house, he couldn't stop looking at me. Even after a year or so, every time he passed by me, he would touch me somewhere or the other. Sometimes he would even come into the kitchen and touch me, or when his mother's back was turned, he would grab me, but never hard, it was always a gentle touch. I used to wait for his touch during the day, dream about the time when he would come back to office and grab hold of me when we were alone and run his hands all over me.'

'Men,' said Arti, giggling. 'They are all like that. Even your father ...'

'Mummy!'

'What did I say?' asked Arti, mock-innocently.

Seema hugged her mother. 'Mummy, Mummy,' she said. 'My Mummy.'

'Look,' said Arti when she had disengaged herself. 'He is coming. He wants to be with you. These are two big things. Listen to me, I have seen a few more years than you have, met a few more people than you have. Whatever the reason for their being together might be, the truth is that when a man and a woman are in bed, there come individual moments that are threads, that, one after the other, over the days and the years, tie the two of them together. Only an animal can ignore those moments, and no one can deny their existence.'

Seema nodded, but the sadness had returned to her eyes.

'This is good news, Bitiya,' said Arti, firmly. 'Today he is coming to sleep with you. Tomorrow he will come and take you back. Trust your mother. I know.'

Through large picture windows designed to give those inside the library a soothing view of the manicured lawns outside, Naresh could see Mr Asthana's profile, his face tilted down over an open newspaper. Behind him were racks and racks of books, the gaps between them revealing another set of bright windows at the other end of the room. At the table next to Mr Asthana's sat an old man whose face Naresh faintly recalled having seen in the newspapers several years ago. In front of the man sat a pile of books. Behind him, on Naresh's side of the picture windows, sat two uniformed men carrying carbines, their relaxed body language evidence of the fact that their function was not so much to protect the old man as to serve as a reminder that he was a personage important enough for someone to have wanted to kill him at some time in the past.

Naresh stood looking at Mr Asthana, then made a silent and entirely futile gesture to attract his attention.

'There's a door on that side,' said one of the uniformed men, not raising his hand, or his gun, to indicate which side he was talking about. Naresh nodded, but didn't move. The man returned to contemplating the perfect carpet of green that separated the library from the lounge and dining room.

Eventually, one of the people at the counter turned towards the window and Naresh, catching his eye, gesticulated towards Mr Asthana.

'There's a door on this side,' said Mr Asthana when he reached where Naresh was standing.

Over tea at a quiet table looking out at the boundary wall bordering the Lodi Gardens, Mr Asthana explained the nuances of the mining project to Naresh.

'There's not much for you to do there,' he said. 'Just keep an eye on things. Make sure the labour doesn't cause problems. Keep the foreigners out of trouble. And if any of those activist types or the media show up, inform me immediately and don't let anyone else talk to them. It's become the fashion nowadays to attack large projects. They don't see the benefit for the people there, they don't want to build anything themselves. All they want to do is to tear things down, file public interest litigations and cause problems for all of us.'

'You don't worry, Asthana Saheb,' Naresh said, trying to sound nonchalant, while growing increasingly disquieted by the unfamiliarity of the terrain his boss was describing. 'I'll make sure there is no problem.'

'This job requires someone who understands how things work,' said Mr Asthana. 'I know I can trust you, Nareshji. Go and meet Khanna. He will get your tickets and put you in touch with our people there. Do you know where Khanna's office is?'

'No, sir.'

Mr Asthana's lip curled up. 'Nareshji, you know where Khanna's office is.'

Naresh hung his head. 'Yes, sir.'

'Just remember one thing, Nareshji. You will gain more by telling me the truth than by lying to me. Do you understand?'

'Yes, sir. I had gone there once. But just once. I was going to tell you about it, but then ...'

Mr Asthana shook his head, an abbreviated gesture that had the desired effect of shutting Naresh up. Picking up his cup of tea, he leant back and sipped it, looking straight into Naresh's eyes as he drank.

'Sir,' said Naresh, averting his eyes, 'there is one other thing.'

'What is it?' asked Mr Asthana, then set his tea down on the table with a clatter and, leaping out of his chair, came out from behind the table with his hands folded and said: 'Sir! How are you? When did you come to Delhi?'

Naresh turned to see that a short grey-haired man, dressed smartly in a button-up suit, accompanied by two younger men, one of whose arms he was holding for support, was walking towards them. Through the old man's thick grey glasses Naresh could see his rheumy eyes light up with recognition when he saw Mr Asthana. 'Bhai, Asthana. I was just thinking of sending word to you.'

Asthana bent from the waist and grasped the hand the old man put out shakily towards him. 'Sir, I have also been meaning to call you.'

'How are things in the ministry?' the old man asked, giving Asthana's hand a shake, but not letting it go.

'They are okay, sir,' said Asthana, putting his other hand over the old man's hand.

'That's not what I have heard.'

'Nothing is hidden from you, sir,' said Asthana, smiling an ingratiating smile.

'Asthana, when you worked under me, I taught you many things. But when I heard the news, I realized that I forgot to teach you one thing. A ministry is called a ministry because a minister runs it.'

'You are right, sir,' said Asthana, nodding his head vigorously. 'I have learnt that lesson now.'

'Have you?'

'Sir, the minister is your party colleague. Maybe you can put in a word for me.'

'Maybe I can,' said the old man, withdrawing his hand after one final shake. 'Come and see me. I am in the usual place, the state guest house. I'll leave for Hyderabad on Monday.'

'I will take an appointment, sir,' said Asthana, moving aside to let the old man pass.

'Useless old fart,' said Mr Asthana, returning to the table and looking over his shoulder as he spoke. 'The party high command kicked him upstairs, gave him a governorship and threw him out of Delhi once they were done with him. What can he do for me?'

'But, sir, you just asked him if he could ...'

'I asked him for help to make him feel good about himself. Both he and I know that no one in Delhi listens to him any more. Anyway, what were you saying?'

'No, nothing. Just that ... do I have to go alone?'

'Alone? Of course not. I told you earlier, rent a nice big house there for yourself and your wife, the company will pay for everything.'

'No, sir. I meant someone to work with me.'

'Work? What work?'

'Just to help around the office. To organize the papers and do the typing.'

'Oh.'

'I was thinking I could ask Pinki to come along.'

'Pinki? Our Pinki?'

'Yes.'

Asthana's brow furrowed. 'But why will she want to go? She hasn't been suspended.'

'She has no work in the office, sir. She can take leave for a few months.'

'And after that?'

'We can see what happens after that.'

'I don't see ...'

'She can also help with my domestic arrangements,' Naresh cut in, realizing after he spoke that he had made a mistake.

'Why? Won't your wife go with you?'

'No, sir. She doesn't want to leave Delhi right now.'

Narrowing his eyes, Mr Asthana hunched over, then looked back up at Naresh. 'And you want Pinki to play your wife over there?'

'No, no, sir. I was just ...'

'Okay,' said Mr Asthana, straightening up. 'You can take her if she agrees. Your domestic life is your business. But if there is some problem that affects the project, remember that you will have to answer for it.'

'There won't be any problem, sir.'

'Okay then,' said Mr Asthana, beginning to unfold his newspaper. 'Inform me once you have got the tickets.'

Naresh did not stand up.

'Is there anything else?'

'There is one more thing, Asthana Saheb. My son ...'

'Yes, yes, I know. I told you Khanna will get him a job in the Bhan Group's office. Just ask him to go and meet Khanna once.'

'It's not that, sir. Actually he is in some trouble.'

Mr Asthana folded the newspaper and put it down. 'What trouble?'

Naresh told him about the murder, Praveen's disappearance and Passi's visit. Mr Asthana listened quietly. When Naresh had finished he asked, 'What do you want me to do about this?'

'Sir, you know people. You can help him.'

'Don't involve me in all this. There is nothing I can do.'

'Sir,' said Naresh, folding his hands. 'I have no one else to turn to, sir. I have served you loyally all these years, and while I can, I will continue to serve you. If you want to do something, you can, sir. I have a lot of faith in you, sir.'

'Okay, okay,' said Mr Asthana, picking the paper up again. 'I'll see what I can do.'

On the television, a news anchor standing against a projected checkerboard background was bringing a sense of intense urgency to some matters regarding the selection of the Indian cricket team for an upcoming series. File photographs of various cricketers flashed on the screen, accompanied by captions laden with question marks.

'They make a big drama out of everything,' Naresh said.

Seema's gaze remained glued to the television. Arti did not look up from her magazine. Ashok's eyes flicked from the television to Naresh, then to Seema, and then back to the television.

Conversation had been strained over dinner, despite Arti's fussing over Ashok even more than usual. Seema had appeared distracted. Naresh had kept quiet, although it had been clear to everyone else that he did not approve of Ashok's staying over. The visit was, after all, explicitly for the purpose of sexual intercourse. And even though Ashok and Seema were married, the idea that his daughter was to have sex in his own house, and that he was forced to confront this fact, made Naresh feel soiled. His critique of the TV anchor's cricket coverage was the first thing he had said since Ashok arrived.

The news had moved on to footage of the opposing cricket team arriving at Delhi airport and being garlanded when Ashok belatedly decided that Naresh's comment had broken the ice. 'Babuji,' he said. 'There's something I wanted to tell you.'

Naresh turned his face towards his son-in-law.

'I talked to someone I know about that sub-inspector, you know, Passi.'

'Passi?' said Naresh, sitting up, then, in a grim tone, his eyes on Seema, 'who told you about Passi?'

'Why are you looking at her?' Arti cut in, putting her magazine down. 'I told him.'

Naresh glowered at his wife. 'Hmph,' he said and turned his face back to the television.

'Why shouldn't I tell him?' asked Arti. 'He is our son-in-law after all, like a second son to us. If we can't turn to him in times of need, who can we turn to?'

'Anyway,' Ashok said, 'I found out something interesting. Passi has been transferred to Narela, just two days ago.'

'Really?' said Arti. 'Does that mean …?'

'He has been removed from this murder case,' said Ashok.

'Did you hear that?' Arti asked her husband. 'Ashokji had him transferred off the case. We are so lucky to have such a powerful son-in-law.'

'No, no, Mummy,' Ashok said. 'I didn't have him transferred. In fact, when I asked my contact about Passi, he said, I don't know what this Passi has been up to, but everyone seems to be talking about him these last few days. First the sudden order from above, then the way he was made to give up his charge and asked to report to Narela the very next day. Now you are calling up to ask about him.'

'So what happened?' asked Arti. 'Did he tell you?'

'No,' said Ashok. 'He didn't know. In fact, he started asking me: why are you interested in Passi? What has he done? I had to give him some excuse and get rid of him.'

The unexpected disappearance of an adversary who had grown in his imagination every day since he first appeared left Naresh feeling like he had woken up in his own bed from a long nap taken at an unusual time of day, disoriented and disconnected from what were clearly familiar surroundings. His mind refused to unpack the implications of what Ashok was saying. Just one single phrase kept sounding in his head.

'Passi is transferred?'

'Yes, Babuji. That's what he said.'

'Are you sure?'

'This person is very reliable. I have done him a few favours over the years. He wouldn't lie to me. Besides, I was only asking him for some information.'

Naresh stood up. He walked to the kitchen and poured himself a glass of water. The mechanical familiarity of the task helped clear his mind. He walked back into the living room, the glass of water still in his hand. Arti's eyes went down to the glass, then back up at her husband. Seeing her look down reminded him that he was thirsty. He emptied the glass in one long gulp.

'Give me that,' said Arti, getting up and taking the empty glass from her husband. 'Are you feeling all right?'

'Yes. I'm okay.'

'This is good news. Isn't it?'

'I don't know. What is the guarantee he won't try to blackmail me even now?'

'He won't,' said Arti.

'How do you know?' snapped Naresh. 'You just say whatever comes to your mind.'

'If he does,' said Ashok, 'tell me. I'll do something about it.'

'Ashokji will help us,' Arti said.

Naresh glared at Arti. Then, bringing his face and his voice under control, he said, 'Thank you, Ashokji. You have given us a piece of good news.'

Ashok smiled and tilted his head to the right as if to say, you're welcome.

'But we are so greedy,' said Naresh, and the warmth that had suffused his gratitude, fake as it had been, left his voice, 'that we want another piece of good news.'

'Babuji!' Seema exclaimed.

'Now stop all this,' Arti said.

'I'm not talking about a child,' said Naresh, still looking at his son-in-law. 'That is not so much in man's hands as in God's. At least, it is not in this poor Naresh Kumar's hands. I am just asking when you will take your wife back to her house, that's all.'

Ashok stood up and faced Naresh. He folded his arms across his chest and, in Arti's eyes, became the powerful government official who was to be feared, who was to be supplicated to, whose benevolence was to be sought, who was never to be crossed. Naresh was not able to entirely free himself of the view Arti had of Ashok but, buoyed by his anger, saw him as the errant son-in-law, the one responsible for his daughter's unhappiness, a young man who had something to answer for. Seema saw the folding of his arms as a gesture of self-preservation and, forgetting in an instant that this man had still not told her when he would take her back, walked across to him and turning to her father, with her husband half-obscured behind her, said, 'That is between him and me, Babuji, you don't need to worry about it.'

Nonplussed, Naresh looked at his wife. But Arti was smiling and Naresh realized that she was moved by Seema's defence of her husband. She was not on his side.

'Hmph,' he said and turned to leave.

'Babuji,' Ashok's voice came from behind Naresh. 'It is also your business. I am answerable to you.'

Naresh turned back.

'You don't have to …' said Seema, but Ashok silenced her with a gesture.

'My mother is not a bad person,' Ashok said, in a measured tone. 'But she has become obsessed with the idea of a grandchild. And somehow the idea that Seema is to blame for this situation has taken root in her mind. If I take Seema home right now, against her will …'

'Sarlaji doesn't want Seema back?' Arti asked.

'There will be a problem,' Ashok continued. 'I go to office in the day, I cannot watch over the situation morning and evening.'

'You are right, Ashokji,' Arti chimed in.

'I'm trying,' said Ashok, still addressing Naresh, 'to convince her that this is not anyone's fault. It is a problem we all have to solve together. All of us. Including her daughter-in-law. Including the woman I married and brought to her house as my wife. The woman who now has as much right to be in that house as I do or she does. But Babuji, you have seen the world, so you know – there are some people who cannot be forced to change their mind. You can only hope that their inner goodness will force them to see what is right and what is wrong. I know my mother is one of those people, I have known it for a long time. But I also know that she is a good person. I have patience. I can wait for her to see that what she is doing is wrong. And my wife, your daughter, also has that patience. She can also wait for her mother-in-law to welcome her back, not because I insist she welcome her back, but willingly, and not just willingly, but happily.'

Naresh looked at Seema. Tears were flowing down his daughter's cheeks. But Naresh could see – even in his angry and disturbed state – that her eyes, fixed on her husband's face, were full of a kind of tranquillity. She was nodding in agreement with what he was saying, but she didn't seem to be hearing anything he said. She was just moving to the music of her husband's voice.

'Pinki?' asked Arti, putting the phone to her ear.

'Namaste Bhabhi,' said Pinki. 'It's me.'

'Yes, yes, of course,' said Arti, the natural affection she had for her husband's colleague flowing into her voice. 'How are you, Pinki? I haven't heard from you for a long time.'

'Yes, Bhabhi. Sometimes it happens like that. We all get occupied in our own lives.'

'Of course, Pinki. I could have also called you. Now tell me, how are you?'

'How is Nareshji?' asked Pinki, deflecting her question in a way that convinced Arti that there was something else that Pinki wanted to talk about.

'You know how it is, Pinki. Staying at home doesn't suit him. Now there is some new thing about working on a project in the Northeast.'

'In the Northeast?'

'Yes. Mr Asthana is supervising one of Mr Bhan's new projects there.'

Pinki had learnt early after joining Mr Asthana's office that there were certain things that Naresh hid from her. She had never confronted him over his reticence, learning over time that there were some documents she was not supposed to look at and that there were particular meetings she was not supposed be curious about. And while she appreciated the fact that Naresh's secretiveness was actually a way of protecting her, she had never completely approved of what went on in the office.

'He shouldn't get further involved with those people, Bhabhi. Look at the trouble they have caused already.'

'I know. I told him clearly, you go if you want to, but I'm staying in Delhi.'

'Then?'

'Then what? He is saying that he will say no, but he may go for an initial tour there, just to keep Mr Asthana happy.'

'Are you sure he will say no?'

'I don't know. But if he says yes, then I won't go. The children are here, our life is here. What will we do there?'

'But who will look after him there, Bhabhi?'

'You have to ask him that question,' said Arti, sounding exasperated. 'Anyway, forget about all that, tell me how you are?'

'Bhabhi, I wanted to talk to you about something.'

'Yes, of course. Tell me what it is.'

Pinki didn't say anything. Through the humming of the phone, Arti could hear her take a deep breath. 'Why don't you come over here, Pinki? Drink some tea with me and we can talk.'

'No Bhabhi,' said Pinki, then stopped.

'Why?'

'It's something difficult … umm, I mean, I don't want to talk about this in front of Nareshji.'

'Oh. What is it that you can't talk about in front of Nareshji? Is it some health problem of that kind?'

'No, Bhabhi,' said Pinki. 'It's about Kamal.'

'Kamal? Who Kamal?'

'Kamaljeet. My brother-in-law from Canada.'

'Oh yes. The one who said he wanted to …'

'Yes. That one. He is here.'

'Here? In Delhi?' Where is he staying?'

'In my house.'

'In your house? You let him stay in your own house?'

'Where else will he stay, Bhabhi? He doesn't know anyone else in Delhi. Besides, how could I tell him to stay anywhere else?'

'Hmmm.'

'He's taken Arjan and Mummy to eat chaat and ice cream right now, so I thought I would call you.'

'Yes, yes.'

'I don't have anyone in Delhi I can talk to either. It's no use talking to Mummy. She is treating him like he is already her son-in-law. Fawning over him. Cooking him lunch and dinner, making her special dal halwa for him. And you should have seen all the clothes he brought for her. There are a lot of people from Punjab in Canada, Bhabhi, you get all kinds of suits and chunnis and everything over there. He brought a whole suitcase full of clothes for her and toys and clothes for Arjan.'

'And for you?'

'Me too. He bought me pink material for a suit. I told him, widows don't wear pink.'

'Pinki! Why say such things?'

'Sorry, Bhabhi. All sorts of things go around in my head nowadays. You know, in Punjab there is a saying that the widow wants to remain honest, but the young men of the village won't let her. In my life it seems that the proverb is becoming a literal truth.'

'Pinki. Tell me clearly what is happening? Did Kamal try anything funny with you?'

'What could be funnier than what he has already done, Bhabhi? He calls me from Canada and says he wants to marry me. Then he comes all the way to Delhi and I find him standing at my threshold one night, his beard beginning to turn grey, looking for all the world like my dead husband, his own cousin, the man whose absence has eaten at me every single night since he died. What am I supposed to do?'

'What do you want to do, Pinki?'

'I don't know, Bhabhi,' said Pinki, her voice beginning to choke. 'I really don't know. If I say yes to him, then people will say that there was always something between the two of them and now that the husband is dead, it is out in the open. My husband will become a laughing stock and he isn't even alive to defend his honour.'

'But who will say all these things? The people in your village? Let them talk. You don't have to listen to every dog that barks.'

'You're right, Bhabhi. I don't. But I do have to listen to the voice inside me that tells me I am betraying his memory by even thinking of agreeing to Kamal's proposal. What do I tell that voice, Bhabhi?'

'If you know that you can't say yes, then why don't you say no?'

'But Bhabhi,' said Pinki, then stopped. Arti could hear her sobbing at the other end of the phone.

'Pinki, my Pinki,' said Arti, tears pricking her own eyes. 'Don't cry, Pinki. What use is crying?'

'Bhabhi,' said Pinki, whimpering as she spoke. 'My body betrays me.' She gasped as she said this, then gasped again.

'Pinki, Pinki,' Arti called. 'Listen to me, Pinki.' But all she heard was a series of thuds as the phone slipped from Pinki's hand. Then the line went dead.

6

THE ROOM WAS DARKENED ONCE THE PROJECTOR CAME ON. The black leather chairs grew blacker and the dark wood panelling grew darker. The delicate, and clearly expensive, china tea cups glistened in the lambent light reflected from the screen.

'Will you eat something, Nareshji?' Khanna asked, interrupting the young man in a smart grey suit who stood at the opposite end of the long table, an infrared pointer in hand.

'No, no,' said Naresh.

'Eat a little something. It is almost four and this presentation will go on for at least half an hour.'

Naresh didn't protest and Khanna, having waited a split second to see if he would, pressed a button on a stylish phone that sat on the table and, over speakerphone, instructed the kitchen while Naresh and the suited man waited.

The young man in the suit spoke in English, his accent indicating that he had been educated at an expensive school. Watching the slides laden with information that was either irrelevant to his role or Khanna had already given him, Naresh realized what was going on. Khanna was trying to tell him that his status had changed yet again. From being powerful as an adjunct to Mr Asthana, he had gone to being nobody when the suspension order had come and now, the benevolence of Mr Bhan, Khanna was suggesting, had made him important again. The chicken sandwich lying on the table, tastefully presented with french fries and steamed broccoli on the side, ketchup separately in a little ceramic bowl; the coffee, a strong pleasing smell coming from it, had a thick head of foam on it and came with two small, rich biscuits; all these confirmed Naresh's conjecture.

Naresh had been in positions of power, even if it was reflected power, for long enough to have begun to believe that the mastery he had on the world around him was of his own. Now, faced with Khanna's generosity, he felt resentment. This new importance that sprang from the person of Mr Bhan, and could be withdrawn at that one man's pleasure, was disagreeable. It made him feel small, especially since it was conferred on him by Khanna, a person whom he had once considered inferior in position to himself.

'Nareshji,' said Khanna, cutting into his reverie, 'you haven't eaten anything. Try the chicken sandwich, our kitchen makes it particularly well.'

There was something in Khanna's tone – Naresh would have been forced to call it kindness if he had to name it – that made Naresh look up at him. He knows, thought Naresh, the realization coming to him with a start. He knows that becoming who I have agreed to become is not easy for me, and he is trying to show me the benefits, trying to make it a little sweeter. And this realization made Naresh look at Khanna anew, made him feel something like gratitude for this man whose well-meaning actions were only making him feel even more wretched than he had felt when he entered through the glass doors earlier that day.

The sandwich remained uneaten through the presentation, so Khanna, whose inability to take no for an answer had probably brought him to where he was, persuaded Naresh to at least accompany him to lunch. Sitting in the back seat with Khanna as Khanna's driver drove through Gurgaon, fancy malls and hotels alternating with construction sites and stand-alone houses, Naresh, who had been here more than once before, found himself wondering for the first time when all this had appeared and who had created this city that resembled no other city he had seen. Only occasional sights betrayed the Indian provenance of this gleaming township: the small tea stall under a tattered piece of tenting, the cycle-rickshaw pushers slowly pedalling consignments of furniture up the side of wide roads, the piles of steel reinforcement bars sitting outside makeshift shop-fronts.

At the restaurant, Khanna helped Naresh navigate a menu full of exotic names, asking him at first if he liked pasta, then struggling to explain what pasta was – 'it's like noodles in different shapes' – and finally just telling the waiter to bring the penne in marinara sauce with chicken.

'I've had to learn all these things, Nareshji,' said Khanna, sheepishly, once the waiter had left. 'Sometimes we have to take people to places like this where there is no roti-sabzi on the menu.' Before Naresh could begin to unravel why this was one of those times, Khanna continued: 'There was something I wanted to tell you, Nareshji. Well, not exactly tell you, I am not allowed to. I asked Mr Bhan, can I tell Naresh Kumarji, he will be happy. But Mr Bhan always says that one of the founding principles of his success is: don't reveal a plan till nothing can stop you from executing it.'

Naresh nodded his head, not in agreement, but because Khanna had, like an orator expecting applause, paused after pronouncing Mr Bhan's principle.

'There are some discussions going on,' said Khanna, a conspiratorial smile on his face, 'that might end with your suspension order being revoked.'

'Really?' asked Naresh, blood rushing to his head. 'Are you sure?'

'Who can be sure of such things, Nareshji? And please, don't mention this to anyone, not even your wife. But there are some discussions going on.'

'Between whom?'

'What does it matter between whom? As long as the end result is good, all these things don't matter.'

Naresh's head felt woolly and heavy. He regarded Khanna with bemusement, unsure of what to say. 'When will it be revoked?' he asked finally.

'That I can't say. People like us can't make these things happen, nor can we predict when they will happen.'

'But,' said Naresh, thinking more clearly now, 'then what is the use of my going to the Northeast? If the order is revoked I will have to rejoin the ministry.'

'What is have to, Nareshji? Who can make you join or not join if you don't want to? And if you do, then join. I know Bhan Saheb well enough to know that he will have no problem, either with you leaving, or finding a person to take your place.'

As Khanna spoke, Naresh's elation at the prospect of being reinstated began to ebb. The thought of not being able to go to the Northeast grew in his head, and he began to feel cheated and trapped.

He carefully donned an annoyed tone and said, 'What is the point of going for two or three months and then coming back?'

'If you don't want to go, don't go.'

I shouldn't have said that, thought Naresh.

'But it may be more than two or three months.'

'You're right,' said Naresh, relieved that Khanna had offered him an opening. 'Who knows when it will happen.'

Khanna smiled at this response and, for a moment, Naresh thought that he knew that Naresh's annoyance had been fake, and that he really wanted the job in the Northeast. How could he know what I want, Naresh checked himself, when I myself don't know what I want?

The food came and the two of them ate silently for a while. Naresh had just begun to enjoy the garlicky taste of his pasta, when Khanna exclaimed, 'Oh yes, I almost forgot one other thing.'

Naresh looked up from his plate.

'In fact, this is probably even more important for you than the other news. I am also a father, Nareshji, so I know.'

'A father?' Naresh asked, apprehension growing within him.

'Yes, yes. Two sons. Thanks to God and Mr Bhan's kindness, both of them are very well settled now, one in America and the other in Mumbai.'

He knows about Praveen, thought Naresh. Mr Asthana must have told him. Page after page of his life was opening out to Khanna, nothing was hidden from him. Naresh had, since he had decided to take the job in the Northeast, been feeling vulnerable and powerless in front of this man. Now, he felt helpless.

'But even your son, Nareshji, is in good hands.'

'Your hands? I mean is he in Mr Bhan's hands?'

Khanna laughed. 'That's not what I meant.'

'Then?'

'Mr Asthana asked me to look into the problem you mentioned to him. You know, the problem with the girl. So I asked around a little bit and found out a few things.'

'What did you find out?'

'I'm telling you, Nareshji, why are you so impatient? It seems your son is an associate of Yadav's – do you know O.P. Yadav?'

'No.'

'Really? If you don't know him, then don't worry. Let me explain it to you this way: Yadav has done favours for everyone who is important in Delhi.'

'What kind of favours?'

'Hmmm. Maybe it is best to say they are small favours. Very small favours.'

'I don't understand.'

'Look Nareshji,' said Khanna with the air of a schoolteacher talking to a particularly slow student. 'There are big favours that can lead to factories being set up or land being bought and sold or contracts being given. And then there are small favours. The favours that last a day. Or maybe, I should say, a night. Yadav does those kinds of favours. And while everyone knows that he does favours for everyone, no one knows what favour he does for whom.'

'But ...'

'And your son, Praveen, works for Yadav.'

'Works for him? What does he do?'

Khanna was about to say something when a waiter came to their table and refilled their water glasses. By the time the waiter left, it appeared to Naresh that Khanna had changed his mind about what he was going to say.

'What does it matter what he does? The main thing is that he is Yadav's man and Yadav will protect him.'

'So this girl who died was …'

'Nareshji,' Khanna cut in, 'why go into all that?'

'But if Praveen is …'

Khanna held up his hand and stopped Naresh. When he spoke, his tone was stern. 'I am telling you to let it go, Nareshji. Sometimes it is better to know less rather than more.'

'You are right,' said Naresh, nodding slowly, his gaze that had earlier been fixed on Khanna's face, now on his empty plate.

'Your son will not be harmed if he is with Yadav. And, besides, we are also with you.'

'Thank you, Khannaji,' said Naresh, forcing the words out of his mouth.

'That driver is going to go to jail for this murder.'

'But the girl … What about the girl? Who actually …? Did Praveen …?'

'Nareshji, I don't expect this kind of behaviour from you. I have told you already that the driver is going to jail for the murder. Why ask questions whose answers don't help you?'

'You are right,' said Naresh, thinking, for the first time, of the girl who died, wondering how her parents must feel.

'Now tell me, would you like something sweet to finish with?'

As Naresh was deciphering the dessert menu, a fair-complexioned woman wearing pants that stopped midway down her shins – shoulder-length hair, dark glasses up on her head – came into the restaurant with two children shepherded by a slim dark girl. They occupied the table next to Naresh's in a clamour of voices, the children wheedling and whining, the girl pacifying and the woman whispering admonishment.

Naresh looked up. His eyes were drawn to the woman. The fair complexion, the slightly curved nose, expressive eyes, they all looked familiar to him. I've met her somewhere before, he thought.

'Have you decided what you want to order?' Khanna cut in, making Naresh turn with a start.

'Why don't you just order something, Khanna Saheb?'

While they waited for dessert to come, Khanna talked about this and that and Naresh nodded along, his eyes drawn repeatedly to the woman at the next table. Where would he have met someone like her? Perhaps at Mr Asthana's house. He had been there a few times when there were visitors, refined men and women wearing expensive clothes. But if he had seen her there, he couldn't place her face; so familiar and yet so different from the faces he saw everyday. And then one of the children said something and the woman's frown vanished. A smile came over her face and the mystery was resolved: this woman was a stranger, he had never met her before. But if her hair had been longer and if she had worn it plaited, if she had no make up on, no dark lipstick, no blush on her cheeks, if she wore a salwar kameez instead of pants and a shirt, if those dark glasses were not there, she would look exactly like Pinki.

Pinki's skin felt like a feather was running lightly over it. The sensation rippled outwards, onto her arms, flowing down to her hands. Emerging through the tips of her finger it leapt across to her thighs and, gathering strength, moved down to her knees. She turned and adjusted the covers, but the feeling refused to go. It just cycled back to her neck and began its downward journey again. This had been happening to her at all times of day and night since Kamaljeet had arrived. It would catch her unawares. Why is this happening? she would ask herself. Why is my skin playing tricks on me? Why is my mind playing tricks on me?

Next to her on the bed, Arjan lay deep in sleep. His small mouth, shaped just like his father's had been, was open. At the other end, Pinki's mother was snoring gently.

She had given up her room for Kamaljeet, taking her dead son-in-law's place in Pinki's bed. Pinki reached out to touch her son but, realizing that her hand was shaking, decided not to. Slowly, quietly, she slipped out of bed, tucking Arjan in as she got up.

In the kitchen, standing over the stove, Pinki felt the steam rising from the boiling water play against her face, softening it, wetting it, warming it. Her skin relaxed. Some lines from the Guru Granth Saheb came through her head: when hands and feet are dirty, water can wash away the dirt, when clothes are stained with urine, soap can wash them clean, but when the mind is filled with sin, only the Name can clean it. She bowed her head and shut her eyes. Her hand went to the dupatta on her head and pulled it up a little further, an action repeated so often that it occurred in a realm that lay beyond that of the voluntary. Prayer filled her head. Her lips moved silently along.

When the tea was ready, Pinki poured it into a mug and, warming her hands on it, took it into the living room. She switched the light on and found Kamaljeet sitting there with his eyes shut.

'Kamal?'

His eyes opened. From across the room, Pinki could see that they were red. He had been crying.

'Kamal,' said Pinki, putting the tea down and going over to where he sat. 'What happened?'

'Nothing, Bhabhi,' he said, wiping his eyes. 'Nothing.'

'You couldn't sleep?' asked Pinki, sitting down next to him.

'No.'

'What happened, Kamal?' asked Pinki, her voice tender and soothing, the voice of a mother whose child has cried more than any child should cry.

'I, I ... I was,' said Kamaljeet, his voice thickening as he spoke. 'I was thinking of Harki Veerji.'

'Oh, Kamal,' said Pinki, reaching instinctively for his hand, stopping before she touched it.

'I can't believe it, Bhabhi,' said Kamaljeet, his body racked with sobs. 'I can't believe he is gone.'

'I couldn't believe it either, Kamal,' said Pinki, taking hold of his hand now. 'I couldn't believe it either for a long long time.'

'You know, Bhabhi,' said Kamaljeet, rubbing his face with his hands, 'you know what he was to me.'

'I know, Kamal,' said Pinki, taking his hand in both her hands and rubbing it.

'He taught me so much. He taught me gilli-danda, he taught me how to swim, he taught me how to climb trees, he taught me how to be with other people, he taught me the difference between right and wrong.'

'He taught us all a lot,' said Pinki, bringing his hand up to her mouth and kissing it.

'And you know the best part: It never felt like a lesson. He never said, put your foot here or hold this branch like that. He just did things the way they had to be done, then turned to me and said, now you do it. He always made me feel like I could do whatever he did. And if I fell or cut myself, he never said that I had done it wrong.'

'He was like that.'

'And do you know, you and I are probably the only ones who knew him well enough to know this quality of his, to know his generosity, to know that he was really what a man should be.'

'There are others. Nareshji respected him a lot. But it's true, what you are saying, perhaps no one knew him as well as you and I did. That is something we have in common.'

Kamaljeet shook his head. 'But what does it matter now, who knows and who doesn't know. It's just a memory. A memory of a dead man. It lives in my head, in my heart, today, and in yours. Then one day we will die and this memory will die as well.'

Pinki opened Kamaljeet's hand and looked at its mess of lines. Many many hours of holding a steering wheel had darkened the skin at the base of his forefinger. She kissed the callus. He pulled his hand back towards himself, but she did not let it go. Instead, she took it in a stronger grip and rested her cheek on his palm.

'Bhabhi,' said Kamaljeet, holding her wrist with his other hand, and beginning to slide his hand out from between her hands and her face. 'I don't want to replace Harki Veerji in your life. I can't replace him, I know that, and I don't want to.'

Pinki, who had begun to feel calm for the first time in days, let his hand go and raised her head. His solemn pronouncement sounded funny to her. Men, she thought, these men. And this one isn't even a man, he is just a boy. Only a boy would think that one man can replace another man in a woman's life. Suppressing a smile, she looked into his face and saw that young man again, the one who had been a playmate to her in those early years. The grey in his beard felt painted on, the beginnings of wrinkles around his eyes seemed to disappear. She wanted to pull his head to her chest and console him, but she didn't because she realized that it would emasculate him. Instead she reached for the hand he had reclaimed, took it firmly and brought it back to her face. She smiled now, her eyes twinkling, and kissed the hand again.

'What happened, Bhabhi?' asked Kamaljeet, disoriented.

'Shhh,' said Pinki. Playing with the fingers of his hand, she contemplated her options. Then she took his hand and placed it on her breast.

'Bhabhi!' Kamaljeet exclaimed, his hand jerking back like it had touched a live wire.

Pinki's smile deepened. She reached out and stroked his bearded chin. Her fingers played against his lips. Kamaljeet's eyes closed. His body shuddered. 'Bhabhi,' he whimpered.

Pinki stood up. She moved forward and took his turbaned head in her arms and brought it to her chest. He rubbed his face over her breasts, bringing his open mouth to where he thought her right nipple might be. Wetness from his tongue spread over her kameez and, as the feeling filtered through layers of clothing, she threw her own head back.

Getting off the sofa, Kamaljeet took her in his arms and, with a fierceness born of long waiting, pressed his mouth against hers. The feeling of his moustache and beard against her face took Pinki back to a time she had thought would never come again. Her knees weakened and her entire weight fell on Kamaljeet's strong arms.

When she regained the use of her legs, Pinki separated from Kamaljeet. She took his hand in hers and turned towards the door.

'Bhabhi?'

'Come.'

Kamaljeet had wanted Pinki for years, unknowingly at first. Soon after he had been forced to admit to himself that he wanted her, he had also been forced to accept that he had wanted her from the time he had first met her. And now, faced with her body, the body he had imagined and pictured in his head for a very long time, he found himself overwhelmed. His memory of the years of wanting but not being close to getting brought tears of self-pity. His feelings for this woman whom he did not just desire but also admired transmuted into a kind of euphoria. And his arousal, cutting through everything, became rapture. But for all the ferocity that Kamaljeet tried to summon up, their lovemaking was overtaken by tenderness, a tenderness that arose from Pinki, that had been born all those years ago, when she had sat and played cards with this young man and brought him into the circle of her affection. Her embraces sandpapered the edges off his passion. And he began to move in time with her gentle rhythms. Her touch made his body feel liquid. Her kisses were astringent, and lovely, on his skin. Kamaljeet had been with women before, but never with one he had known for so long, never with one who had been a companion and a friend. And so, unlike in those few unsatisfactory encounters, the arousal he felt with Pinki was warm and rounded. It came on slower and rose to levels higher than he had ever known. Bhabhi, Bhabhi, Bhabhi, he said – he couldn't call her anything else – until it became an incantation. Kamaljeet floated in that moment, his eyes rolling back, the passage of time at a halt in his head, his body, freed from the control of his mind, pushing him towards release, a soft, incandescent release that lingered for minutes.

Later, when Kamaljeet regained his sense of where he was, he saw that Pinki was looking at him with a mischievous, content smile. Seeing his eyes open, her smile broadened. It was a smile that a mother would give a child, not one a woman would give a lover. And when he saw that smile, Kamaljeet knew instantly that this first time he had made love to Pinki would also be the last. And he knew that this was how it should be. 'Bhabhi?' he said, hoping that he was wrong.

'Go back to Canada now, Kamal,' said Pinki. 'I won't be coming with you.'

The Himalayan ranges came into view minutes after the plane took off from Delhi: an unbroken chain of glistening whites and cool greys. The sight, commonplace to the regular traveller on the Delhi–Kolkata sector, took Naresh by surprise. The shining jagged edges of the horizon had a mesmeric effect on him, relaxing the tight muscles of his neck, filling him with a sense of contentment. He luxuriated in a feeling of rightness, something he had not felt for a long time. This was the correct thing to do, he thought. Everything would be fine. He would eventually convince Arti to come along with him. And if she didn't, Pinki would be there to look after him and perhaps, if the project went on for long and Arti did not come, he could convince Pinki that it made sense for her to take Arti's place in his life. But this last thought made him uneasy. The idea that he might actually make a life away from Arti, the woman who had been his companion for decades now, brought a twinge of sadness with it. He focused again on the distant ranges in an effort to block out that feeling. And, as if it were planned just for him, the angular magnificence of Everest came into view and, for a moment, everything else shrank before it.

On reaching the town closest to the project site, after a long journey full of mountainous wonders, Naresh found that work had already begun, even though several permissions were still to come. Within the first two days he realized that Mr Asthana had been right: there was nothing for him to actually do. The operation was very well organized and could work without his interference. But he wanted to assert his newly found authority and the natural way to do it was to inspect every aspect of the project and to meet the people working on it. This meant driving for hours to remote parts, Lakhpa, the site supervisor hired by the Bhan group, informed him; places where he would have to camp overnight at least, perhaps stay for a few days if the weather was bad. Naresh showed some irritation at this suggestion, because he assumed Lakhpa would expect him to, but inwardly he was overjoyed. He called Arti and told her that his original plan to stay for three or four days would have to be changed. If he didn't demonstrate to Mr Asthana that he had made an effort to familiarize himself with the project, Mr Asthana would see through the charade, he told her. She complained a bit, but it is easier to object to someone's going away when they are not yet gone, and so there was little she could do.

'I'll call you when I have coverage,' Naresh told her and, having said that, shut his phone off and relieved himself of the responsibility of having to call her.

The first thing Naresh did was to take over all the files from Lakhpa. He bought a cupboard that could be locked and put them in it. Then he sat down with him and worked out an itinerary to visit all the project's locations. Enjoying having someone to instruct, he instructed Lakhpa to collect provisions for the trip and to send word that he was coming, surmising that if word was sent that he was coming, the people he was going to meet would assume that he was someone important.

The ten-day excursion through hilly terrain turned out to be the single most uplifting experience of Naresh's life. They drove most of the day, stopping to eat meals that Lakhpa cooked on a kerosene stove he had carried along. After a meal they rested for a while, sometimes taking walks through beautiful quiet forests. They stopped at the sites in the evening, eating and drinking by campfires. At the first stop, Lakhpa hinted to Naresh that he could organize a woman for him, but Naresh refused and the offer was never made again. During the day, Naresh met the engineers – some of whom were from the Ukraine – and the labour, and asked them what questions he could about the progress of the work. At first, he was surprised by the deference they showed him, then he began to revel in it. A lifetime of bowing and scraping before his betters had prepared him well for this opportunity to be the one who was bowed and scraped before. In the afternoon, he would use Lakhpa's phone to call Mr Asthana in Delhi and tell him about the site he was visiting. Mr Asthana did not seem to know much about the nuts and bolts of the project, nor did he seem to care, so the primary purpose these phone calls served was to establish Naresh's status as the man from Delhi, and that purpose was enough for Naresh to continue making them. Initially, Mr Asthana had been surprised that Naresh had decided to extend his stay in the Northeast, but he had not forced the issue after

Naresh had strenuously argued that it would be better if the people here felt that he was committed to the project. And with that matter successfully resolved, Naresh settled into the rhythm of the tour, invigorated as much by the mountain air as by the distance from his life in Delhi, a life that had begun to feel like it was someone else's, not his own.

Naresh returned to headquarters filled with resolve. The inconveniences he had encountered here – the cold, the strange food, the languages he didn't understand – seemed minor compared to the beauty of the place. The calm and quiet, the relaxed pace at which things moved, all these seduced him. He was too worldly to think that living here would not require major adjustments, but a man who has rarely been on holiday can sometimes confuse the exhilaration of discovering a strange and lovely new region with the mellower contentment of coming upon a place that might be home. Back from his ten days of enchantment, he went about organizing his future life here with purpose.

After some searching, he found a house that appeared perfect. It was shaped like a U, with two sets of rooms on each arm separated by a common living area. The back was open and afforded a magnificent view of snow-capped mountains. Pinki and her family could stay in one set of rooms, he thought, and I could stay in the other. There would be no need for two kitchens, I could eat along with them. But the question of sleeping quarters was only the first and most basic one. Pinki's son would need to go to school, her mother would need to see a doctor about her knees from time to time. Naresh went to Lakhpa with these problems. Lakhpa, who had learnt in the course of conversations over the past ten days that Naresh's children were both grown up, was somewhat puzzled at his query about schools in the area, but he told Naresh about a missionary school that was about half an hour away by road. When asked about orthopaedic facilities in the area, he asked Naresh who they were needed for, but didn't press the question when he realized Naresh was prevaricating in answering it. There were basic medical facilities at their headquarters, he told Naresh, but it was a one-hour drive to anything like a proper clinic with a doctor. This piece of information, innocuous in itself, served to puncture Naresh's bubble somewhat. He started thinking of how Arjan would adapt in a place where hardly anyone spoke Hindi, where the children looked and behaved very differently from his friends in school. Pinki's mother too had a group of friends she met in the park every evening, women of her own age, Punjabis mainly, with whom she spent a couple of hours gossiping. There would be nothing like that over here. Who would she spend time with? The questions came faster and faster, the answers grew less and less convincing, and Naresh's euphoria slowly bled away.

Walking through the forest late one afternoon, Naresh found himself on a narrow ridge between two hills. Away on the other side, high peaks were ranged in the distance.

They gleamed white in the strong sunlight. Standing there, Naresh thought for the first time how it would be to come away to this place on his own. These three weeks had been easy enough. His food was taken care of. He had the companionship of Lakhpa and the few others who worked at the site. There was a television with all the channels he had in Delhi. And apart from that, there was this silence, this fresh air, these tall trees and these mountains. Why did he need Pinki? And this thought led him to a puzzling realization: he had spent some time trying to figure out how Pinki and her family could be accommodated here, but he had not once thought of what would happen if Arti actually agreed to come with him. Standing there, alone in front of the mountains, he took out his phone and switched it on. He looked down at its screen and waited for it to come up, transfixed by this small dark artefact that appeared to be the single thread connecting him to the life he had left behind. The phone came on finally. Its battery was still half-charged, but there was not a single bar of network coverage. He shut the phone off and put it back in his pocket. Why did he need anyone? he thought. Why couldn't he live here by himself? He turned and started walking towards the camp, the path leading him back through the forest. Perhaps the second stage of his life was over, he thought. Maybe it was time now to step away from the world of human relations and move towards the forest, free from encumbrances.

A light breeze started, cold and bracing across his face. The trees sighed. A cloud came over the sun and the dappled shade he had been enjoying turned dark. Naresh's step quickened. He could live here alone, he said to himself. But what about Arti, could she live without him? He would provide for her, he always had. That would not change. And Praveen? He had Yadav to protect him, he had obviously found his own way. Seema? She had her husband. They didn't need him there. He could live here now. He could live here alone. This one line – he could live here alone – sounded again and again in his head as he walked through the forest, pulling the collar of his jacket up to keep the cold out. And with every repetition of this line, the realization grew within Naresh that it was not true. There was a part of him that wanted to renounce the world he had built for himself, there was no doubt about that, but there was another part of him that was not ready to let go of that world. He was not ready to go to the forest. He was still a householder.

Ashok came over one evening, a few days after Naresh left. Arti calculated that it was only three weeks since he had spent three nights at their place, but she didn't point this out to Seema, or to Ashok. Instead she cooked dinner for him with her customary enthusiasm and sat and chatted with her daughter and son-in-law after dinner as if it were the most normal thing in the world for him to be staying the night with his wife in his in-laws' house. In the morning, she had his tea ready early, at the time he liked it, and made his favourite gobhi parathas for breakfast. She didn't ask him whether he would come back that evening. She saw her daughter blush when Ashok said goodbye that first morning, and her mother's intuition – the same instinct that had told her, all those years ago when Seema was a baby, that her child was hungry or unwell – told her that he would be back.

The fourth evening in a row when Ashok came over, Arti asked him if his mother was okay with his spending his nights here. Ashok parried the question at first, then said, 'Sooner or later she will have to understand.' What exactly he wanted his mother to understand he did not specify, but Arti understood what he was saying and she exulted silently at his statement. What a man this Ashok was, she thought. First, he had brought news of Passi's transfer and Arti had found her fears about Praveen fading away, assuming that her powerful son-in-law would take care of her son. And now he was willing to defy his mother for Seema's sake. Inclined by nature and conditioning to idolize her son-in-law, Arti began to think of him as some kind of demigod. Sometimes she wondered if he wasn't doing something dangerous, if this form of confrontation with his mother wouldn't end in some kind of conflagration, but when she saw Seema smile to herself over her tea, or jump up when her phone rang and run into her room clutching it to her ear, Arti's doubts became insignificant and a warm feeling came rushing through her, sometimes driving her to tears.

Ashok's daily visits distracted Arti from Naresh's absence. The first two or three days after her husband left, Arti had felt abandoned, and angry at Naresh. His phone calls had been short and abrupt in those first days, and when he had said he was going to be out of coverage for ten days, she had not had the time to tell him that she felt betrayed by his departure and that his extension of his time in the Northeast was only making it worse. But then, the day after his last phone call, sitting in front of the TV with Seema, she suddenly realized that she was relieved that Naresh had gone. Her guilt at feeling this way about her husband was leavened by a deeper pragmatism. She knew that all these years they had spent weekdays apart. On weekends they had been together, but they were either caring for the children or eating meals or even going to watch movies or on picnics. Naresh's suspension had created a gulf of unplanned time together. It had been difficult for both her and him to have to confront each other across this gulf. His moodiness, and her inability to do anything to cheer him up, had worn her down. Perhaps this break was necessary, she thought, the change would do him some good. Some days when Seema overslept, as she sat drinking her morning tea alone, Arti would wonder what Naresh was doing. She tried to picture him walking through forests in a mountainous area. Whenever her mind conjured up the image of Naresh, clad in a woollen scarf and a jacket, his hands linked behind his back, her heart melted. He would be so lost in a place like that, she thought, dwarfed by the tall trees and the hills. Sometimes the fear that Naresh would want to leave for good played on her mind. But her implicit faith in the strength of her marriage and Ashok's visits kept that fear from taking her in its grip.

Seema took her mother shopping a few days after Ashok started coming to their house. She bought a toothbrush, shaving cream, some blades, a few shirts, a pair of pants and some underwear for Ashok. 'He doesn't want to carry a suitcase out of his house,' she told Arti, who agreed with the sentiment vigorously. When they returned that afternoon and Seema took the numerous bags they had acquired into her room, Arti realized that Ashok had effectively moved in. He still spent the weekends with his parents, but come Monday evening, he would be back and he would stay till breakfast on Saturday. Arti wondered sometimes what the conversation was like at his house on those two days in a week, but Ashok never mentioned his parents or any displeasure they might have expressed.

Arti started looking forward to evenings with Ashok. Every other evening, he would suggest that they go out somewhere. Arti would always feign reluctance, he would always insist, as would Seema, and Arti would demur for an appropriate amount of time, then happily go along. They would go shopping for handicrafts and textiles at Dilli Haat; on a Thursday he would take them to the dargah in Mehrauli to listen to qawwali; one day he took them all the way to the Red Fort for the sound and light show, stopping off in Bazaar Sita Ram on the way back for some of the best chana-bhaturas Arti had ever eaten. 'Delhi has many nice things,' Ashok would say, 'we just don't enjoy them as much as we should.' Those few weeks that Naresh was away turned out to be the best holiday Arti had ever been on. And she didn't have to leave home for it either. An odd sequence of circumstances had taken her into a new household, the two men in her life replaced by this third one. It was like a thick woollen shawl had been thrown over her shoulders on a cold winter night. She wrapped herself in the fabric of the relationship her daughter and son-in-law shared, and she was warmed and soothed by it.

Some days, instead of venturing far from home, at Seema's suggestion, the three of them would go to the nearby market for chaat. Seema and her mother both loved golgappas, happy to eat eight at a time, enjoying the ritual of standing around with their steel bowls, waiting their turn while the man put boiled potatoes into the fried shells, then filled them with spicy water and handed them out one at a time. The first few weeks they went once a week, but then one week, Seema wanted to go two days in a row. Arti didn't think much of it the second day, but on the third day when Seema said she was craving golgappas again, a beautiful suspicion arose in Arti's mind. She looked carefully at her daughter and thought she saw a new glow on her face. That glow could just be Seema's happiness at having her husband with her or, and this thought sent flutters through Arti's stomach, it could be because of a change within Seema's body. Arti didn't want to say anything, didn't want to suggest a test. If the test came out negative, the bubble of contentment the three of them were living in would burst.

A few days later, Ashok told Arti that he wanted to take Seema to meet his family's astrologer. The next morning, he took half a day's leave from the office and the two of them went away. When Seema returned, she deflected Arti's questions about what the astrologer had said. She appeared distracted and somewhat tense, and so Arti didn't press the matter. Ashok returned home late that day, past seven. He rang the bell not once, or twice, but three times in quick succession. When Arti opened the door, she saw him standing there, an open box of sweets in his left hand, two stapled sheets of paper with something printed on them in his right hand and a broad smile on his face.

'Mummyji,' he said. 'Congratulations. You are going to be a grandmother.'

'Is that what the astrologer said?' Arti asked.

'No, Mummyji,' said Ashok, handing her the papers. His right hand was now free to pick a laddoo out of the box, which he duly began to stuff into his mother-in-law's mouth. 'Sometimes a blood test can also tell the future.'

7

THE NAMEPLATE AFFIXED JUST ABOVE EYE LEVEL WAS FLECKED with brown from the last time the door had been painted. The owner of the name that was emblazoned across the centre of the plate, Naresh Kumar, stood in front of the door, suitcase in hand, staring at the golden lettering. His mind wandered back to the day he had gone to collect the nameplate, to the time when he had brought it home for the first time to a different, smaller, house and shown it to his children. They were still children then. How excited they had been! Clapping, they had cheered him on as he slid it across the door, centring it from the sides, deciding the perfect height, knocking nails into the wooden door, and finally stepping back and hugging them before opening the door and walking through it and further into the kitchen to drag Arti out to force her to admire this small rectangular piece of wood that proclaimed Naresh as the head of the family that lived behind this door. His eyes still fixed on his own name, Naresh put his suitcase down and rang the doorbell.

'Babuji!' It was Seema who opened the door. She ran forward and hugged her father. 'Mummy! Mummy! Come quickly, Babuji is here.'

'Why did you ring the doorbell?' asked Arti, appearing in the doorway, wiping her hands on her sari. 'You know the door is not locked at this time.'

Naresh realized that he had known that the door would be open, he just had to turn the handle and go in, like he always did. Why had he rung the doorbell? Since the time the disembodied voice of a flight attendant had welcomed Naresh and his co-passengers to New Delhi's Indira Gandhi Airport and informed them of the outside temperature, Naresh had been unable to postpone thinking of the questions Arti would ask him. All the way back in the taxi, he had struggled to formulate the answers he would give. And now here he was, completely exposed by a small gesture, faced with an unanswerable question: why would the master of the house ring its doorbell? His mind had betrayed him. He had fallen straight through the crack. 'I thought you might be alone,' he mumbled.

'Sit,' said Arti, turning away. 'I'll bring some tea. Seema, put the suitcase away.'

'Mummy,' said Seema, taking hold of the suitcase, 'don't forget to bring the laddoos he brought. We need to sweeten Babuji's mouth.'

'No, no,' said Naresh, hurt by his wife's abrupt behaviour and, consequently, charmed by what he thought was a ritual his daughter had invented to welcome him back. 'What is the need to sweeten my mouth? I haven't been away for that long.'

'No, no, Babuji, it's not for that,' said Seema, not noticing in her excitement that Naresh's face fell at her casual dismissal of his fake protestations. 'It's for something else.'

'What is it?' said Naresh, gruffly. What could be more important than your father returning home after almost six weeks, he thought to himself.

'Let Mummy come,' said Seema, her eyes shining. 'I want her to also see your face when I tell you.'

While Seema waited for Arti to return, Naresh waited for Seema to ask him about his trip to the Northeast. His eyes wandered around the room, resting in turn on the expensive sofa bought in Ghitorni, the television ensconced in the cover Arti had embroidered herself, the dining table that had been made to order at one of the shops on Panchkuian Road. Outside the window, across the lawn, he saw the evening's lights come on in a house. A woman, about Arti's age, was going around her living room straightening things. Her husband must be about to return from office, he thought. He had met the husband downstairs, once or twice. What was the man's name? Bhalla or

Taneja, something like that. Which department was he in? Maybe Fisheries, thought Naresh, then realized that his mind was wandering.

'Here's your tea,' said Arti, putting his cup down with a thud. 'And here are your laddoos.'

Seema picked up one of the laddoos and began to push it into her father's mouth. The aroma of congealed ghee hit Naresh's nose a moment before the sweet taste entered his reluctant mouth. 'Congratulations, Babuji,' said Seema, her voice rising in excitement. 'You are going to be a grandfather.'

For a moment Naresh could focus on nothing but the sensation of his teeth grinding the soft morsel of laddoo. His mouth kept moving even after the small bite he had taken had slid down his throat.

'Did you hear what I said, Babuji?' asked Seema. 'I am going to have a baby.'

'That is very good news,' said Naresh slowly, turning at the sound of her voice. 'Very very good news.'

Seema threw her arms around his neck. Naresh flinched at her first movement, then, once she had already taken him in his grasp, he turned gingerly and put one arm around her back.

'Babuji,' said Seema, her voice breaking, 'I'm going to have a baby, Babuji.'

'Don't cry, Beta,' said Naresh, patting her repeatedly on the back and saying the only thing he could think of saying. 'Don't cry.'

Arti walked over to her daughter and took her by the shoulder. 'Your waiting is over, Beta,' she said. 'Your patience has borne fruit.'

Seema hugged her mother tight, sobbed a few more times, then straightened up. 'It's all because of you, Mummy,' she said. 'Without you, I would have fallen apart.'

Arti gestured to Naresh to get up and comfort Seema, but he did not move. Instead, he looked away, the turning of his head sending a wave of anger through his wife.

'What's wrong with you?' asked Arti, separating herself from Seema. 'Why are you sitting there, acting like you're watching some other family's daughter crying her eyes out on TV.'

Naresh stood up. 'Nor has anyone here asked how I am, or how I have been for these last two months,' he said, his voice trailing off as he spoke, as he realized the pettiness of his complaint.

'It's difficult to call a switched off phone,' said Arti curtly.

Naresh found himself mumbling something incoherent in reply to a statement to which he knew he had no reply.

'Hmph,' said Seema. 'All the two of you want to do is have your own fights. I am sick of it.'

Her parents turned to look at her, but she was already on her way out of the room.

Later that afternoon, Naresh sat and watched Arti unpack his suitcase, separating the clothes she felt needed to be washed from the ones that needed ironing. Their bedroom didn't look like he had not been in it for almost two months. Maybe because she always keeps it neat even though I leave things lying around, thought Naresh. This house doesn't seem to bear any signs of my not having been here. And for the first time since he had entered the house, he thought of his time in the hills of the Northeast, of how he had felt in those last few days, how much of an outsider. He let out a deep sigh.

'What happened?' asked Arti, putting a shirt on a hanger.

'You have every right to be angry with me.'

'I am not angry with you,' Arti said, and it was true. Ashok's visits had drained away her anger within the first couple of weeks. Naresh's absence, her son's continued absence, these had both become minor irritants. The reversal in Seema's life made Arti feel like nothing was wrong with the world, and the small things that were out of place would soon fall back into place again.

'When Seema told me about the baby, I was really happy.'

'No, you weren't.'

'Let me finish. I was happy, but not really happy, not from the inside. You were right, what you said earlier, it seemed like it was something that mattered to someone else, not to me.'

'I know.'

'But why, Arti? Why should it be like that? I also wanted it so much. I took her to AIIMS, faced humiliation from Bhutani, prostrated myself in front of her in-laws. I always wanted only one thing: her happiness. And it's here now. Then why?'

The pain in his voice made Arti stop and turn towards him. She saw her husband sitting on a chair, his hands in his lap, his head down. 'Listen,' she said, in the gentlest voice she could muster. 'Don't be so hard on yourself. We all wanted what you wanted. But maybe that wanting lay heavier on your shoulders because you are the father. You are the one who has to make everything all right.'

'But I couldn't make anything all right.'

'You tried. You tried as hard as you could.'

'And it was not good enough.'

Arti went to where he sat and put her hand on his shoulder. 'Don't punish yourself like this. Human beings can only try. Your duty is only to try.'

Naresh took her hand, held it for a moment, then let it go. 'You are right,' he said, more to pull himself together than in agreement with her. 'All we can do is try.'

Then Arti sat down on the bed across from her husband and started telling him everything that had happened in the last two months. She told him about Ashok's visits, about the blood test. They had been to the gynaecologist and asked for an explanation. How had this suddenly happened? The doctor had explained that fallopian tubes sometimes get blocked because of infections and can simply reopen once the infection has passed. Perhaps that was what had happened here. 'We didn't push the question too much,' Arti said. 'After all, the important thing is that she is pregnant.' She told Naresh about how Ashok had surveyed various doctors and various hospitals. There were some hospitals in Delhi now that specialized in childbirth. They were expensive, but Ashok had said that money was not a consideration. He had taken Seema and Arti to one in Greater Kailash and they had registered there. 'What facilities!' said Arti. 'The rooms are like a five-star hotel's rooms.' She told him that she hadn't heard from Seema's in-laws yet, but Ashok had indicated to her that they were just waiting for Naresh to return, then they would come themselves and take Seema home.

Naresh sat quietly and listened to her narration, snorting in disgust at the doctor's cluelessness, widening his eyes appropriately at her description of the five-star hospital, nodding inscrutably when Seema's in-laws were mentioned. But inwardly, he was struggling to convince himself that all this mattered to him. He knew the role, he had played it for so long that he could play it without even wanting to. But he felt removed from that role today, like he was an actor up on stage in front of a packed house who just didn't feel like saying his lines.

Eventually, Arti ran out of things to say. 'So tell me, how come a four-day trip got extended to two months?'

'Mr Asthana was very keen that I see all the locations,' said Naresh, the rehearsed answer spilling out. 'And travelling there takes a lot of time. Each trip took three or four days and there are twelve different sites.'

'Anyway, that's done now. When are you going to tell him that you can't take the job?'

'I'll go and meet him in a day or two.'

'That's good,' said Arti, getting up. 'Okay, I have to go and cook now. We have been talking for a long time.'

'Yes. You go.'

She turned and walked away, leaving Naresh sitting there, repeating to himself the answers he had prepared about how things were in the Northeast and what he had seen and done there.

In the distance, through the tall tree trunks, Naresh could see a row of snow-clad mountains. There was a clearing at the end of the forest, a place where he could stand and look at the mountains, but he walked and walked and he couldn't seem to reach it. Somewhere behind him, there was the sound of voices that grew louder and louder. He could make out Seema's voice and Arti's and there was a male voice, a young man. But before he could identify the voice, his eyes opened. He turned to the side table and saw it was almost eight-thirty in the morning. The voices he had heard in his dream were still sounding in his ear. They were coming from the living room. He got out of bed and went towards them.

'Babuji!' said Praveen, putting his tea down and standing up when his father entered the room. 'Babuji, I'm back!'

Naresh's head swayed back. His eyelids fell, then opened again. He stood motionless for a moment, a moment in which Seema and Arti both stood up. Then he lunged forward, his right arm raised and pulled back.

'Babuji!' Seema cried, moving forward to stop him. But before she could get to him, Naresh had reached Praveen and slapped him hard across the face.

'You bastard,' Naresh said, his hand pulling back to launch another blow. 'You pimp. You dog.'

Praveen put up his hands to protect his face. Naresh's slaps bounced off them as he repeatedly tried to hit his son. 'You murderer, you pimp, you bastard,' Naresh kept repeating, pushing his wife and daughter away with his left hand as his right hand kept rising and falling.

Finally, Praveen lowered his hands. His left cheek was pink. His eyes were red. He put up his hand and intercepted his father's arm. 'Enough. That's enough.'

The day passed in uneasy silence. Naresh took his afternoon tea into the bedroom. At dinner, he said nothing and did not look anyone in the eye. The next morning, when he picked up his tea cup and stood to leave, Praveen got up and barred his way.

'Babuji,' he said, folding his hands. 'Please at least listen to what I have to say. After that, you can do what you want. If you want to throw me out of the house or if you want to break my bones, I will accept whatever you say.'

Naresh looked at Praveen's face for the first time since his son had caught his arm in mid-air and arrested it with the strength of his youth. Then he turned back to the table, put his cup down and sat.

'Babuji, I don't know what you have heard or what you think. But I swear on my mother that I didn't kill Rekha.'

Naresh heard him pause, but he didn't say anything. Arti got up.

'Mummy, I want you to hear this too. And Seema, you too.'

Arti sat down.

'Babuji, maybe you have heard me mention Yadav once or twice.'

'Hmmm,' said Naresh, shaking his head in disapproval.

'Maybe, while I have been away, you have heard about Yadav from other people also.'

'Hmmm.'

'Yadav is a very powerful man, Babuji. He knows everyone in Delhi. He has done favours for everyone. The kind of favours they want to keep secret.'

'I know.'

'What kind of favours?' Arti asked.

'There are many different kinds of things. One of them is that he provides important people with girlfriends.'

'Girlfriends!' snorted Naresh. 'Why don't you just say prostitutes?'

'Whatever you want to call it, Babuji.'

'But what has this got to do with you, Beta?' asked Arti, the quaver in her voice indicating that she already knew the answer to the question.

'I help him find the girls,' said Praveen, lowering his eyes.

'What?' exclaimed Arti. 'How can you do such a thing? Do you know what they call people who do such things?'

'I know.'

'Then why, Beta? You have a job, a well-paying job. And we have always provided for you. Why would you do such a thing?'

'Someone introduced me to Yadav,' said Praveen, still not raising his head. 'Yadav told me that call centre girls are always interested in making some extra money. And the truth is, Mummy, those girls are like that.'

Seema stood up. 'I don't want to hear any more of this,' she said. No one stopped her.

'Offer them some money, a new mobile phone, a laptop, some jewellery,' said Praveen, a smile beginning to play at the corner of his lips, 'and they will agree to anything.'

'Don't talk nonsense,' said Arti. 'Those girls may be whatever they are, that doesn't mean you should become their, their, their ...'

'Pimp,' said Naresh.

'But Mummy, if I don't do it, someone else will. What difference will it make to the world?'

'But, Beta ...'

'No, Mummy. I understood one thing very early in my life. There are two types of people in the world, those who have power and those who don't have power. And I also knew that if you get a foot into the door of power, it is your own responsibility to push your way in.'

'What is he saying?' said Arti, turning to her husband. 'I don't understand what he is saying.'

Naresh gestured to her to keep quiet. 'All that is okay. Tell us what happened to the girl.'

'That night, Yadav had asked me to take my best girl to a very important person's farmhouse,' said Praveen.

'Whose farmhouse?' asked Naresh.

Praveen gave a grunt of laughter. 'Let it be, Babuji. Let's leave names out of this. He is a very very important person. So I called Rekha. She was the most popular one of them all. Beautiful face, great figure and she was really ...'

'Really what?' asked Naresh.

Praveen smiled slyly, gave a sideways glance at his mother, then said, 'She was a really good worker.'

The pain that flashed on Arti's face caught at Naresh's throat.

'An hour after I dropped her off at the farmhouse, I got a call from Yadav,' Praveen said. 'I don't know what happened in there, what sort of thing was going on, but somehow, in the process of ... somehow he had killed her. It was an accident, Yadav said, and I believe him. And even if it wasn't, what could I have done about it? I went rushing over there. Yadav was there too. We had to take her body and get rid of it. Poor Rekha. She had been so alive, so full of joy, so beautiful. And there she was, eyes shut, lipstick smeared over her face. Her body had gone cold by the time I got there.'

'Hey Ram,' said Arti. 'Hey Ram.'

'Anyway,' said Praveen. 'We did what we had to do. Then Yadav told me to leave Delhi immediately, to make sure my SIM card was destroyed and my mobile phone was crushed to bits and discarded. He gave me the names of a couple of his friends in and around Manali. He gave me some money and then I left.'

'Why didn't you go to the police?' asked Arti.

'Babuji,' said Praveen. 'What kind of question is she asking?'

'Forget it,' said Naresh. 'Go on.'

'Yadav said he would take care of it,' said Praveen. 'And he did. There were some people nosing around after me, but he fixed them.'

'I know,' said Naresh.

'You know?' asked Praveen. 'What do you know?'

'A sub-inspector called Passi had come here,' said Naresh. 'He asked me for money.'

Praveen laughed out loud. 'Don't worry about that worm. He has been fixed. If I had known he had bothered you, I would have gone and slapped him a few times myself.'

Despite himself, Naresh smiled with pride. Then, seeing Arti's expression, he hastily erased the smile from his face.

'Then?' asked Naresh.

'Then what? Nothing. Yadav has taken care of it. He told me last week that it is safe for me to come back to Delhi, so I am back.'

'But what about the girl?' asked Arti.

'What about the girl, Mummy?' asked Praveen, in the tone of a parent talking to a slow-witted child.

'What about her murderer?'

'The driver is going to be prosecuted,' said Praveen. 'There's a very strong case against him.'

'But he didn't kill her,' said Arti. 'Did he?'

'No, he didn't,' said Praveen. 'But her parents think that he did. If he gets convicted, they will get the justice they want.'

'Justice,' said Arti, separating each syllable of the word.

'Yes, justice,' said Praveen.

'This is not right,' said Arti. 'This is not right.'

'Mummy,' said Praveen, his voice taking on a darker tone, 'you cannot say anything about this to anyone. I have told you because you are my parents, so you should know. But no one else can know.'

'She won't tell anyone,' said Naresh.

'Because even if she does, or you do,' said Praveen, turning to Naresh, 'no one will believe you. The only thing that will happen is that you will get into trouble and I don't know if I will be able to protect you.'

Arti stood up. She folded her hands and closed her eyes. Her husband and her son watched as her mouth moved in prayer. Then she opened her eyes and said, 'I have to go to the temple.'

'Mummy ...'

'Don't worry about your secret,' said Arti. 'I won't tell anyone anything. I carried you in my stomach. I fed you my milk and comforted you when you cried. I won't do anything to harm you.'

Praveen got up and made to hug Arti, but she evaded him and walked out of the room.

'Babuji?' said Praveen, turning to look at Naresh.

'Tell me one thing,' said Naresh. 'How did you know that Yadav wouldn't frame you for the murder? How were you so sure that some other scapegoat would be found?'

Praveen smiled a broad smile. He sat down and pulled his chair closer to his father. Putting his hands on Naresh's knees, he said, 'I know a lot about Yadav's dealings, and he knows that I know. That's why I knew he would not betray me.'

Naresh put his hands over his son's and tried to remove them from his knees, but Praveen turned his palms upwards and grasped his father's hands. 'You see, Babuji,' he said. 'I have learnt some things from you.'

Naresh had learnt, maybe from his father, maybe from the world as he saw it, that a man must prepare himself to face whatever befalls his family. And he could honestly say that he had spent his working life following that maxim. He had never tried to tabulate all that he had done for his family, every fight that he had fought – but, he now thought, if he did, then he would probably find that every moment he had counted as significant in his life was present in that reckoning. And this was the way he had wanted to live his life. He had always known this, even if he had never expressed it to himself or to anyone else. There was nothing to be gained from asking why he had wanted this, no question of wondering if one can really want something if one doesn't know why one wants it. In his life, in his days, he had wanted to provide for his family, of this he was certain.

It was not just something he had thought – in fact he did not recall ever explicitly thinking it – it was something that he had lived out. He had cultivated no bad habits. He had never indulged himself at the cost of his family. Some envious people said he was corrupt, that he used his position and his proximity to Mr Asthana to make money, but he knew that he had never asked for more than what he felt he needed to secure his family's future. Was that not his responsibility as a father and the head of the family? He had not been born rich or privileged. The job his father had pushed him into gave him certain opportunities. It had been his duty to take them. And in the years that had gone by since he first bought his wife a kadhai that would not burn her hands, he had done his duty as well as anyone could have asked him to: he had educated his children, he had bought his wife every domestic amenity she could think of, he had married his daughter off in style to a well-placed man who, he had thought, could keep her in the way a man must keep his wife. And to do all this, Naresh had struggled with many things in the years since he had left the protective umbrella of his father's house – he had fought off jealous colleagues, dealt with children's illnesses, manoeuvred hard for promotions and postings, sometimes successfully and sometimes not. But one thing he had never struggled with was doubt.

Now, when the unforeseen whose shape he would not have been able to predict some months ago, the unforeseen whose presence each human who has lived has sensed, had come, Naresh had been found wanting. His suspension had made him painfully aware that the solid ground he thought he stood on was, and always had been, prone to crumbling at the whim of the powerful people to whom his fortunes were tied. And suddenly he had been beset with doubt. It was as if the day he had surrendered the identification card that allowed him to enter his office, he had also handed in his certainty and the unstated principle by which he lived. Just like that he had been reduced to nothing, a useless housebound man, unable to shelter his family from the multiple storms that struck it. And instead of standing his ground in the face of those storms, he had chosen to flee. Mr Asthana had provided him with an escape route and he had taken it.

Despite what he had said to Arti, he had gone to the Northeast with the intention of preparing himself to move there. And although the weeks he had spent there had frightened him and had made him painfully aware that he was not capable of life on his own, they had also calmed him. He had left the Northeast thinking that his only option was to do battle with the problems that lived in

Delhi. He had accepted that he would have to fight this fight, that he would either win it or lose honourably. But he had returned to find that both his children were okay: the battle he had run away from had finished before he could return to the battlefield. The storms that had been visited on his children had not destroyed what came in their path; they had passed on their own. And in doing so, they had robbed him of the opportunity to redeem himself. While he had been walking through the hills and forests of the Northeast, an opportunity that he had not even realized he needed had come and gone, never to return. It had seemed like a minor thing when he was away, extending his stay there by a week at a time. And it wasn't as if he had been gone for years. But the consequences of being away for those few weeks would last for years. Ever since Praveen had told him that he was not in trouble over the girl's murder, Naresh had found it difficult to look Arti in the eye. He had been rescued by circumstances this time, he had been lucky, but Arti knew now that he was vulnerable, he was fallible. How could he live with her, knowing that she knew this? There was only one option: he had to turn around and go back to the Northeast.

Going back to the Northeast meant that he had to convince Pinki to go with him. There was no other way. He needed his meals taken care of, his clothes washed and ironed, and someone to look after him if he fell ill. He needed to buy vegetables and spices and hand them over to someone who would cook them for him; he needed to provide comforts to people who depended on him. He needed to be the head of a household, successfully this time.

If Pinki came along, he would not make the same mistake again, he would not let her down the way he had let Arti down. He would be a good father to Arjan, a dutiful son-in-law to her mother. This time he would make sure that he could handle whatever befell them. The thought struck him that Harkirat, who was more of a man than Naresh could ever hope to be, had, nonetheless, abandoned Pinki. He had died, leaving her helpless. And it was he, Naresh, who had stepped in and helped her find her feet after he had gone. He, Naresh, who had eventually trumped Harkirat in a competition that neither of them had been aware they were in, by continuing to live. It would not just be a second chance for him, it would be a second chance for Pinki as well.

Since he had returned, he had not called Pinki or gone to see her. It was not only that he thought she might have agreed to marry Kamaljeet, it was also that when he decided that he could not move to the Northeast, he had the irrational feeling that he had broken a promise made to Pinki. With Kamaljeet out of the way, with his own life in Delhi now unliveable, Naresh was ready to fulfil the promise he had, in his own head, made to Pinki.

8

STANDING IN FRONT OF THE BUILDING HE HAD WORKED IN for years, the building that he had been among the first occupants of, Naresh looked up. It didn't look as new as it had when he first arrived here to take charge of the keys and supervise the shifting of Mr Asthana's files. The red sandstone facade was showing wear at its edges. Streaks of black had formed below the air-conditioners that marked the important offices. He stood in front of the building, hesitating, and, perhaps because it was the first time he had not just walked in through the doors without lingering outside them, he saw the building in its entirety, he felt the presence of the hundreds of people who worked inside it. An array of faces passed through his head, snippets of their life stories attached to them. And for one brief unexpected moment, his heart ached at the thought of what these people must have suffered in their lives and what they were yet to suffer.

Mohan Lal, who sat behind the desk at the reception office where entry passes were issued, was on the phone when Naresh entered the room. His neck jerked up when he saw Naresh. He stood up, dragging the phone off the table in the process. The base of the instrument swayed, suspended from the receiver that was still at Mohan Lal's ear, clattering against his table. 'Sorry, sorry. I will just call you back.'

'How are you, Mohan Lal?'

'Nareshji,' said Mohan Lal, bending down to try and reunite the two parts of the phone instrument, then abandoning the project and straightening to greet Naresh. 'How are you? How is Bhabhi?'

'Everything is fine.'

They stood facing each other wordlessly for a minute. Then Mohan Lal remembered his manners. 'Will you have some tea?'

'No. Make me a pass.'

'But Nareshji,' said Mohan Lal, embarrassment contorting his face, 'it's … I mean … you are …'

'I know. But I am here to meet someone. Suspension rules do not prohibit me from entering the building if I am here to meet someone.'

'No, I wasn't saying … I mean, yes, yes,' said Mohan Lal, sitting down and hurriedly pulling the entry register towards him. He wrote out Naresh's name, then picking up a dog-eared copy of the ministry directory, copied out Naresh's phone number and address. He filled 'personal' under 'Purpose of Visit'. His pen halted then, hanging in the air above the 'Whom to Visit' column. He looked up.

'Shrimati Pinki Kaur.'

'Yes, yes,' said Mohan Lal, scribbling as he spoke. Then he opened the entry pass pad and scrawled everything he had entered in the register on to it. Tearing off the pass, he handed it to Naresh and said, 'Are you sure you won't have a cup of tea?'

'Shouldn't you call Pinki before issuing the pass?'

Mohan Lal again thrust the pass towards Naresh, his face beseeching him to take it. Naresh took it.

'Bhabhi is fine?' asked Mohan Lal. 'And the children?'

'They are all fine.'

Pinki looked up from her magazine when the door swung open. 'Nareshji!' she said, rising to her feet.

'Pinki,' said Naresh, the sight of her bringing an involuntary smile to his face. 'How are you?'

'You didn't call. You just came like that?'

'I told Mohan Lal to call you … But he didn't.'

'No, I meant …' said Pinki, picking her mobile phone up from the desk. 'Anyway, let that be. How are you?'

'Okay,' said Naresh, his eye landing on the red wax that had been used to seal the keyhole of the cupboard that stood near Pinki's desk. Turning, he saw that the door to Mr Asthana's office was padlocked. The keyhole of the lock had a piece of brown paper taped over it, with a 'sealed' stamp on it. He craned his neck, but he couldn't see the drawers of his desk from where he stood.

'They are also sealed,' Pinki said.

Naresh had a sudden urge to rip the paper off the padlock, to pry out the red wax with his fingernails. His nostrils flared. Letting out a deep breath with some effort, he nodded. 'That is the procedure.'

'Come and sit, Nareshji,' said Pinki. 'Drink some tea.' She opened her flask and poured some tea in a china cup. It was one of a set of four that Pinki had bought for the office the week she had joined, one of a set of four that he had drunk from perhaps a few thousand times.

'Here,' said Pinki, handing him the cup.

Naresh took it gingerly, afraid that he might drop it, shatter it and never be able to drink from it again.

'How was the trip to the Northeast, Nareshji?' asked Pinki, pouring herself a cup of tea as well. 'I thought you were supposed to go for a few days, but you spent two months there.'

'There was a lot of work there. Many sites to visit. And very spread out. It's only when I got there that I realized that a week would not be enough even to inspect one site properly.'

'So, you want to work on this project,' said Pinki, disapproval visible in her eyes and audible in her voice.

'It's a beautiful place. Tall trees, rolling hills, views of snow-capped peaks.'

'Really?'

'Unbelievably beautiful. The air is so fresh, the light is so clear that you never feel like being inside.'

'It must be very nice.'

'Nice? Nice is nothing. It is much beyond nice. When I was there I felt healthy and energetic like I have never felt here. I felt like eating big meals and walking long distances. I never got a headache. Even my stomach seemed to feel better.'

'It sounds very good, Nareshji.'

'For the first time, Pinki, when I was there, I got the feeling that I have squandered my health in this filthy, polluted Delhi. Sitting all day in an office with no windows, under this pale white light, what kind of life is that?'

'But this is our life,' said Pinki, more bewildered than combative.

'It doesn't have to be. There is an option now.'

'Option? What option?'

'This project in the Northeast is different. There is fresh air there, most of the work is out in the open, in the forests and hills.'

'Do you really want to work on this project, Nareshji?' asked Pinki, her brow knitted. 'These people are ...'

'What's wrong with these people? The Bhan Group has helped me when I needed it.'

Pinki sighed. 'Yes, it will be something different.'

'Maybe,' said Naresh, then stopped. There was nothing left to say now except what he had come to say, there was nothing left to do except what he had come to do. 'Maybe ...'

Pinki said nothing. She just sat still with her head tilted slightly upwards, suddenly feeling that she had to brace herself for what Naresh had to say. But Naresh didn't complete the sentence he had started.

'Why have you come here today, Nareshji?' Pinki asked, slowly drawing out the words as she spoke.

'I came to meet you.'

Pinki nodded, not knowing how to respond.

'I was thinking, Pinki,' said Naresh, his head down now, his eyes on his hands. 'There is a lot of work there. And a lot of touring around for me. I need someone to look after the head office while I am visiting the sites.'

'Oh.'

'Do you want to come and work there?'

Pinki rose from her chair. She walked around the desk and pulled a chair from Naresh's table and turned it to face him. He looked at her face as she sat down on the chair, searching it for clues to what her answer would be. She sat, folded her hands in her lap, her head bowed. Then she looked up at him and when he saw the expression on her face – the ache of pity – he knew that she would say no.

'Nareshji, I think of you as a brother. I have always thought of you as a brother.'

'No, no,' said Naresh, his voice made tentative by the clarity of his realization that she would not agree, that she could not agree, that the hope that had brought him here today was entirely baseless, that it had always been entirely baseless, that he already knew somewhere deep inside that it was entirely baseless. 'I was just suggesting that you come and work there.'

'I know what you are suggesting, Nareshji,' said Pinki, her eyes clear, the beginnings of a furrow in her brow. 'It cannot be.'

Naresh's head hung down. 'But you said no to Kamaljeet,' he mumbled.

'Yes, I did,' said Pinki. 'But what has that ...'

'I thought that meant ...'

'That I would say yes to you?'

Naresh nodded.

Pinki reached forward and took Naresh's hands in hers. Her firm grip told Naresh that she had known for a while that he wanted something more from her. It told him that the answer to his question had always been no. And perhaps she had never made it as clear to him as she was making it today because he had been hesitant enough to not ask the question as clearly as he was asking it today.

'I said no to Kamaljeet,' said Pinki, 'not because I wanted someone other than him. I said no to him because I realized that I had already had my time with the only man I ever wanted to be with in my life.' Then she released his hands, got up, put the chair back from where she had taken it and went back behind her desk.

Naresh sat there with his eyes on the ground, his mind slowly clearing of the shame and embarrassment that had filled it a moment before. An emptiness spread through his head as he looked at the floor of what had been his office, a floor that he had never really noticed before, whose speckled concrete greyness felt like it was entering his body through his eyes, moving through the hidden corridors of his soul, settling in remote corners.

As he stared at the floor, unable to raise his head, unable to rise from his chair, Naresh began to feel like he had thrown his last card and still lost. From within him came a directive: surrender! Accept that the rock you are trying to push will not move. A feeling of release came over him – his arms felt limp and relaxed, like sleep was overtaking his body. This was what it felt like to become nothing, he thought.

There was a loud knock on the door, but before either of them could rise, it swung open. Two men, one carrying a set of tools in his hands, walked in. Naresh raised his head slowly and looked at them. He had seen them around the building before, he thought, and that thought sounded in his head like a voice coming from far away.

'We're from Vigilance,' the man without implements said. 'We're here to unseal the office.'

Naresh had been waiting poised at the edge of an expensive sofa – the sofa whose pale imitation had cost him thirty thousand rupees at a Ghitorni shop – in Mr Asthana's living room for almost an hour when his boss came sailing in dressed in a dark suit, his hand at the knot of his tie.

'Nareshji!' exclaimed Mr Asthana in the cheery tones of a man who has recently won a minor victory. 'Good you came. I was going to call you.'

'Asthana Saheb,' said Naresh, leaping up. 'I have some important news for you.'

'Can you wait for a minute?' asked Mr Asthana, not breaking his stride. 'I'm boiling in this suit.' Half a second later, he had disappeared from view, leaving Naresh standing on the Persian carpet with his hand outstretched and his mouth frozen in the process of forming words.

Fifteen minutes later, Mr Asthana returned, freshly bathed, clad in a crisp off-white kurta and pyjama, carrying a pack of cigarettes and a lighter. Settling into an easy chair, he took a cigarette out, lit it, pulled deeply at it, then, as the smoke curled in front of his face, turned to Naresh and said, 'Nareshji, there is good news for you.'

'Sir,' said Naresh, 'I have something important to tell you. Vigilance has removed the seals on your office.'

'Really?' asked Mr Asthana, the half smile on his face revealing that he had not been taken by surprise. 'How do you know?'

'I was there when they came,' said Naresh, immediately realizing that he should have lied instead, maybe said that Pinki had told him.

'You were there?' said Mr Asthana, arching one eyebrow, the amusement still on his face. 'What were you doing there?'

'Sir, I ... I was ...'

'Anyway,' said Mr Asthana, crossing one leg over the other and leaning back, 'whatever you were up to over there, let me tell you that you need not have worried your head with it.'

'Sorry, sir,' said Naresh.

Mr Asthana waved away the apology with one hand, bringing the cigarette to his mouth with the other. 'Enjoy these last few days of your vacation, Nareshji,' he said as he exhaled the smoke. 'From Monday, you have to go back to work.'

'Work? You mean in the Northeast?' asked Naresh, although he knew that Mr Asthana did not mean the Northeast.

'Tch tch, Nareshji. This is not expected of you. I am telling you to get ready to go back to work. You yourself saw Vigilance remove the seals when you were in the office for reasons you don't want to tell me. And now you say this. Since when have two and two added up to five?'

'Sorry, sir.'

'Today is Monday,' said Mr Asthana, stubbing his cigarette out and leaning forward. 'The Inquiry Committee will submit its report tomorrow. Their report will say that they have found no evidence of procedural irregularities in the Port Trust deal as alleged by the anonymous complainant. By Thursday, on the basis of this report, the Minister will authorise the reinstatement of the officer suspended and his assistant. Orders will be issued for the same on Friday. You and I will rejoin on Monday.'

'On Monday,' echoed Naresh.

'One more week for you to relax, Nareshji,' said Mr Asthana, his eyes gleaming. 'And then back to work.'

'But, Asthana Saheb, what about the work in the Northeast? How will I be able to supervise it from here? There are so many sites, so many things to keep track of. Half the places don't even have cell phone coverage.'

'Yes,' said Mr Asthana. 'That's the other thing I wanted to tell you. The project in the Northeast will now be executed by the Vijay Group, not by the Bhan Group. So there is no question of you, or anyone from our side, interfering in it.'

'The Vijay Group?'

'Yes,' said Mr Asthana, a broad smile on his face. 'The Vijay Group.'

'But ... but how?'

'If you live in the water, Nareshji, you cannot make the crocodile your enemy. It's not me who is saying that. This is Babaji's advice. You remember, I told you I went and met Babaji in his ashram near Palwal. It was he who worked out a compromise.'

'A compromise,' repeated Naresh, realization beginning to dawn on him.

'Yes, a compromise,' Mr Asthana said. 'The project in the Northeast goes to the Vijay Group. But the Bhan

Group gets a fifteen per cent stake in the company. In return for that, the Bhan Group gets the scrap metal deal, with a thirty per cent stake in that enterprise going to the Vijay Group. The Port Trust case is dropped, for good, and we further gain by now being in a proper working relationship with our Minister.'

'But, but ...'

'But what?'

'But I spent so much time inspecting the sites,' said Naresh, almost blubbering now. 'I travelled for days and went to every corner, sometimes having to walk for hours.'

'I didn't tell you to do all that,' snapped Mr Asthana. 'You kept saying you want to go here and you want to go there, so I let you.'

'But you knew all along that this was going on,' said Naresh, standing up but keeping his eyes averted from his boss. 'Why didn't you stop me?'

'When the word gets out, it travels a long way. You know that, Nareshji. Besides, I got the feeling that you were going on extending your time there not because you wanted to do the job diligently, but for some other reason.'

Naresh looked up now. Asthana was still sitting in his chair, leaning back in it, regarding Naresh through narrowed eyes.

'What other reason could I have had?'

'And then,' said Asthana, ignoring the question, 'you yourself said that your wife would not come with you. Even if the project was still in my hands, and you could take leave and go, how would you live without your family for so long?'

'No, but ...'

'Oh yes,' said Asthana, continuing. 'There was some harebrained idea of asking Pinki to go along with you. As if your wife would accept that without a fight! So, did you ask her? Did she agree?'

Naresh nodded, then nodded again. 'No,' he said. 'Pinki didn't agree.'

'You asked her?' asked Asthana, incredulous.

'I did.'

In the silence that followed, the sound of a dog barking floated over the hum of traffic from the main road and entered the room. The light outside had faded. Naresh's stomach rumbled and he realized that he had eaten nothing since morning. A feeling of faintness made his head spin, but he shook his head and it passed.

'Nareshji, you used to be different earlier, much more sure of yourself. Something has happened. Over these last few months, I have begun to feel that the faith I have had in your abilities may now be misplaced. What has happened, Nareshji?'

For just one instant, Naresh felt like telling Mr Asthana everything that had happened in these last few months and everything he had felt. He felt like explaining to him that he had never in his life known the kind of uncertainty that he had known in these last few months, never felt like running away before, never felt like he did not have it in him to provide for his family. But this man, with his richly appointed house, his children safe in foreign countries, his access to people like Mr Bhan and Babaji and the Minister, this man would never understand what it felt like to be suddenly shown how close the edge of the precipice was. Besides, he knew that if he showed Mr Asthana the fear that had made its home just below the surface, his boss would have him transferred back to the secretarial pool, where he would have to spend the many years that lay between now and retirement taking home nothing more than the salary he was entitled to, besides having to face the ridicule of those who had been jealous of him, of those who enjoy kicking people when they are down.

'Nothing has happened, Asthana Saheb,' Naresh said, collecting himself and speaking in the most even tone he could manage. 'I have served you faithfully for many years. And I will continue to serve you as well as I always have.'

'Hmmm.'

He is going to get rid of me, thought Naresh when he saw the thoughtful expression on his boss's face. And although some older part of Naresh was saying that this was not a good thing and that he should do something to reverse it, he said nothing. Somehow the fear of losing his place as Mr Asthana's closest minion had departed now, not seconds after it had come. Out of nowhere, he found himself thinking of his pay slip: his basic pay, grade pay, then his index-linked dearness allowance, transportation allowance. If he moved into one of the houses he owned in Delhi, he would also be entitled to house rent allowance. It adds up to a good amount, he thought, especially now that the Sixth Pay Commission's recommendations have been accepted.

'Nareshji?'

'Yes, sir,' said Naresh, snapping out of his reverie.

'What were you thinking about? Did you hear what I just said?'

'Sir, I was just thinking of how to reorganize the files so that this Port Trust kind of problem does not arise again.'

'Hmmm,' said Asthana, but this time with a smile on his face.

'There are some papers that need to be moved around.'

'Start moving them around on Monday itself, Nareshji,' said Asthana, picking up the cigarette and lighter to signal that the meeting was over. 'I know I can trust you.'

'Yes, sir.'

'Where were you all day?' asked Arti, opening the door and finding her husband standing there. She had a metal spatula in one hand. Her sari was tucked in at the waist. Beads of sweat had formed on her forehead. 'You haven't been picking up your phone either.'

'I had gone to meet Mr Asthana,' said Naresh, a long

forgotten thrill passing through him at the sight of his wife standing there, pulled out from the kitchen by the doorbell.

'You haven't brought any vegetables either,' said Arti, wiping her brow with the back of her hand, streaking it with yellow paste.

'You are making pakoras,' said Naresh, a broad smile taking over his face.

'How do you know? I haven't started frying them yet.'

Naresh reached out with one finger. He ran it slowly through the middle of the yellow stain on her forehead. Then he put the finger in his mouth, sucked on it thoughtfully and said, 'Too much salt. Not enough chilli powder.'

'Dhut!' said Arti, blushing. She ran her hand over her forehead. 'Why didn't you tell me there was besan on my face?'

'I thought you were trying some new kind of make up.'

Arti opened her mouth as if to respond to this, then stopped. Her mouth closed, her brow cleared and her eyes looked into her husband's as if they were searching for something. 'You are in a good mood after many days,' she said gingerly, afraid that identifying his mood as good might transmute it back into bad.

'Why?' asked Naresh, annoyance creeping into his voice. 'Am I always in a bad mood?'

'No, no,' said Arti hurriedly. 'Anyway, come in now. Do you want to stand here all evening?'

Naresh walked into the living room and turned all the lights on. 'Where is everybody?'

'Ashok came earlier and took Seema shopping,' said Arti. 'They have gone shopping for baby clothes and to look at baby cots. And a chest of drawers to put all the clothes in. There are so many things to buy.'

'Yes. Children are expensive.'

'And Praveen. Who knows where he is? He never tells me where he is going or when he will be back.'

'Don't worry about him. He can take care of himself.'

'Hmph,' said Arti, turning to go.

'Where are you going?' asked Naresh, reaching for her.

'I have dinner to cook. And also I have to make tea for my lord, and you will want pakoras with your tea, now that you know that there are pakoras.'

'Come here,' said Naresh, a childlike insistence in his voice.

'What do you want?'

'Come here, then I'll tell you,' said Naresh, beckoning her with his hand.

'And who will cook the dinner?'

'Forget dinner. We are all going out for dinner tonight. To your favourite restaurant.'

'Sagar?' asked Arti, turning back, her face brightening at the thought. 'It's been a long time since I ate a nice dosa.'

'Yes, Sagar. Now come here.'

Arti went and sat across from him.

'No,' said Naresh, shifting into a corner of the couch and patting the spot right next to him. 'Come here.'

'What has happened to you?' asked Arti, getting up with alacrity, a smile on her face. 'Why are you in such a …'

'Good mood?' asked Naresh, his voice free of rancour.

'Hmmm.'

Naresh caught her arm as soon as she was close enough to him, pulled her down on the sofa, put his other arm around her and brought his lips to hers. She wriggled for a moment, taken by surprise, then her body relaxed and her face pushed up to meet his. His hand slid down her arm, landed on her hip, then moved back up to her waist, just above her sari. He touched the exposed skin of her midriff. She jumped up. 'It's cold,' she giggled.

Naresh blew on his hand, rubbed it against the sofa, then returned it to where it had been, and just before he took her lips to his lips again, he said, 'Is it okay now?'

In response, she linked her two hands behind his back and pulled him further in.

When they were done kissing, Naresh laid his head on Arti's shoulder and she fiddled with his hair. 'What happened?' she asked.

'Nothing. Nothing happened.'

The sparkle in Arti's eyes deepened into something tentative and concerned. He blinked once, then again, and then his gaze steadied. When they were both younger, Naresh had spent long hours just looking into her eyes. He knew their every mood. Now they were on him, these eyes, and in their soothing darkness were some questions that he knew he would have to answer. But he also knew that the answers to those questions would not, could not, be given in words. And the deeds that would answer those questions could not be planned. But he had the answers, he knew now that he did have the answers to those questions. And this realization came welling up through his body and reached his own eyes, filling them with tears that trembled at their corners.

'Tell me what happened,' said Arti, in a voice so tender Naresh could almost feel it like a hand down his back.

'I met Asthana Saheb today,' said Naresh, choking on the words. 'My suspension has been revoked. I have to join next Monday.'

Arti's eyes widened. Her mouth opened and shut. Then her eyes narrowed and she burst into tears. 'Oh Mother,' she wailed. 'You have heard my prayers.' She lunged forward and buried her head in Naresh's chest. 'I knew it,' she said, over and over again. 'I knew everything would be alright.'

Her tears soaked through Naresh's shirt, her body throbbing as she wept. Naresh enveloped her in his embrace. An incongruous thought came into his head: on Monday he would return to the office. And, unexpectedly, it brought a gentle elation with it.

Arti called Seema and told her to return immediately. Even the wilful Praveen said he would come home when he heard the news. Having made her phone calls, she ran into her bedroom and lit an incense stick in front of her small statue of the Mother Goddess. Then she bustled into the kitchen and put the kadhai on the fire.

'Make some tea also,' said Naresh from outside, leaning forward and picking up the newspaper.

Later, they all sat in the small living room, drinking tea and eating pakoras. Ashok praised his mother-in-law's cooking, as he always did, and his mother-in-law blushed at the praise, as she always did. Seema and Praveen bickered over who got to eat the potato pakoras and who got to eat the onion ones, and Naresh sat back, watching and sipping his tea. The room filled with the sounds of their voices and, in the middle of it all, Naresh sat, thinking that perhaps – no, not perhaps, but surely – there would be a time when he would have to leave all of these people and go away to the place that each one of us must someday go to. But that time was still in the future and he was here right now.

Acknowledgements

The first debt I owe is to my parents, Ajoy and Indira Bagchi, who have taught me honesty and integrity simply by living their lives in the way they know best. After them comes Shrilal Shukla: the moral force of his novels has affected me deeply. I dearly treasure all that my son, Kisho Bagchi, my sister, Anuradha Sural, my in-laws, Vipen and Kuko Kapur, have given me. Dr Bhaswati Ghosh gave me important medical inputs for this book. Amitav Ghosh and Shruti Debi have both been great sources of support. I would like to thank V.K. Karthika, Ajitha G.S. and Shuka Jain at HarperCollins India. And after all, above all, thanks are due to my wife, my true North: Ratika Kapur.